T0196545

The
Spirit of
Catherine

authorHOUSE®

AuthorHouse™
1663 Liberty Drive
Bloomington, IN 47403
www.authorhouse.com
Phone: 1-800-839-8640

Published by AuthorHouse   08/20/2012

ISBN: 978-1-4772-0300-2 (sc)
ISBN: 978-1-4772-0301-9 (e)

Library of Congress Control Number: 2012908464

For my loving grandparents.
A special thank you to Emma L. Hall.

FOREWORD

Before I met Miranda, her father had shared with me what an extraordinary young lady she was. She could sing, act, write, make good grades, have a part-time job, workout at the YMCA, attend church, help with her brother and sister, and at the end of the day, have a great attitude. Before I met her, I assumed her dad was just like any other dad, a little over complimentary. Well, I was wrong. She is far more advanced than the majority of teens today, and she even exceeds most adults. Talk about a young lady who has it all together! Miranda does.

One of the first things I noticed about her, along with her long curly hair, is her sweet, humble demeanor. She is so grateful for the blessings she has been given from God. Miranda realizes that God has His Hand upon her, and to absolutely know this is amazing!

I am involved in a book with seven other women entitled *Now Is the Time* and Miranda was interested in hearing about it. We were talking about it when Miranda revealed to me that she had written a book when she was twelve. I asked her for a copy. Miranda's father had not read the book, and though he had requested the manuscript many times, Miranda was always too busy to get it to him. Being so humble, she did not show much emotion about it and I could not get a clear understanding of the content or quality of the book from either of them. Once I got my hands on it though, I couldn't believe it! This book is more than amazing! It was written by a little girl from St. Louis who writes about pain, sorrows, loss of life, plantations, slavery, and freedom, all at the age of twelve!

I want to thank Miranda and the Holy Spirit for allowing me to be a voice of encouragement and to help Miranda birth her book to the world. I can envision this young woman speaking at schools encouraging other young people to help make a difference in this world. I can see her on television encouraging parents to propel their children to achieve greatness. I could even see Miranda's book as a play on Broadway. How about an Oscar winning movie? Why Not?

Wherever Miranda might go and whatever she might do, I know that she will always allow the Hand of God to be ever present with her. I know you will enjoy reading *The Spirit of Catherine* and realize very quickly that with God, all things are possible for those who believe. Miranda believes and so do I.

Pam Jarrett is an entrepreneur, corporate trainer, life coach, speaker, and author. She is also the CEO of Creative Consultants which works as an agent for speakers, assists in fund raising, and offers personal counseling. Pam is also the founder of two non-profit ministries: Bibles for Teens and Kids Loving Kids.

For information on the non-profits, send an email to **biblesforteens@gmail.com**.

To hear more about Creative Consultants, or reserve personal time with Pam, you may contact her at pamjarrett1@gmail.com.

PROLOGUE

Charleston, South Carolina

Life goes on. It's the three words that dominate my world. It's the three words that forever gnaw on me and huddle over me, replaying over and over and over again. These very words have stayed with me throughout everything. The day after my mother died, when I was crying myself to sleep, my father spoke them harshly to me. In that time of desperate need, my father pointed out that life goes on. And there was nothing anyone could do about it. Nothing to make it better. And he was right.

Life forever goes on as I parade around in my fancy gowns and somber etiquette and horse-drawn buggy, even though with each moment the life inside my soul darkens and collapses, like a lit candle that slowly melts until it burns no more. Inside me I have heaps of melancholy, but life goes on as I endure every moment, every choice of mine that is decided by my father like a map of life laid before me, including every expectation of my father and of society. My life is an endless cartwheel of the same old routine, the same old people, the same old society rules that can't possibly get any stricter. I've learned to accept that I have no say in how my future will go, that it has all been decided for me. What I want is not of any question. I'm just a little girl in a world of business and men and hatred. I'll simply have to wait until the barely flaming candle burns out, whenever that may be.

July 30, 1854

Charleston, South Carolina
Carey Plantation

Milly shook me awake before dawn. I was so tired I could barely function, and my eyelids felt like they weighed a thousand pounds. What could my chambermaid possibly want?

"Missy!" she cried, frantically shaking me by the shoulders. "Missy Catherine! Wake up! There's a fire in the house!"

"What?!" My eyes shot open, and I scrambled to my feet. Milly stood before me, dark skin plastered with sweat and face streaming with tears. I had never seen her cry before. "What are you talking about?"

"I smelt smoke so's I got up and touched the door. It's hot, Missy! There's a fire on the other side! I heard screamin'. We gotta go out through the window."

I felt my forehead and neck, finding them to be sticky with sweat. I grimaced, my senses sharpening as the toxic brusqueness of smoke filled my nostrils. Gray fumes squeezed between the crevices of my door, and Milly screamed. I covered my hands over my ears and sat down again in bed, seemingly in a daze. What would we do? How would we get out? The fire was close now. My body begged and ached for sleep. All I wanted to do was ball up and wrap myself in my covers and shut out everyone and everything. But I couldn't do that. I wanted to live. I needed to live. Didn't I? I angered myself with these contemplations and looked up to Milly, who ran around the room in frantic, purposeful movements. I sat in a daze, staring at her. Her mouth moved, words spilling out in vain, and her eyes pierced me, but all I could do was sit, oblivious to everything. Suddenly her nails dug into the tender skin of my shoulders, and she shook me hard that my head swam.

"You plannin' to sit here and die, Catherine? You listen to me, now. You hear? Listen to *me*. Now I packed some of your nice things and clothes into—"

She cut off when a piercing scream broke through the air. Along with the screaming I heard voices, commands, orders. These voices belonged to black men, slaves of my father's. I heard pots banging, commotions downstairs, in what I suspected to be the heart of the fire. Tears sprung to my eyes suddenly and gooseflesh prickled all over my body, despite the intense heat. I began to cough as the smoke in the room now hung over us.

"We are gonna jump out through the window. You hear me? You hear me?!" Milly released me, and I fell back against the bed. Without another thought, I sprang into action, following Milly's example. The window was

2

practically ancient, along with the rest of the house, and it hadn't been opened in years.

"I need your help. I can't get it open myself." She revealed her hands to me, bruised and bleeding.

The window had been sealed shut by my father in hopes to keep Milly from sneaking out. He had found her one night outside, just by the house, climbing up a rope tied to my window made of stockings. He hadn't beaten her; I'd begged him not to, but he had a slave man nail and board up the window tightly so she could never leave again. Together, Milly and I pulled and yanked on the nails, using every object we could to pry them away from the hinges. Our muscles aching and our minds whirling, we kept on, knowing this was the only way. The tears on my cheeks stung and my temples throbbed, but I used every ounce of vigor I possessed to break the window loose. Finally we'd removed the first plank of wood. I fell to my knees to begin work on the second, and then the third. Milly cried out to the Lord as she pulled and yanked, her fingers a bloody mess. I looked down to my own, seeing them to be almost as bad as Milly's. In disgust I felt my head become light and dizzied, but I kept on until all of the planks had been successfully pried from the window.

The room now reeked with smoke, and we had to squint to see. My eyes burned as if they were on fire, and tears rushed down my face in rivers. Milly frantically tied together stockings and petticoats to serve as a makeshift rope.

"Hurry . . . Milly, hurry," I coughed, dropping down to my knees. She released the window and we both scrambled to our feet, shoving the suitcase filled with many necessary things of mine out first.

"But Papa!" I managed to hoarsely whisper. "Where?"

Milly didn't hear me, and if she did, she wouldn't have answered anyway. She hated the man I called father, for some reason I didn't know. He nailed the window up; that was all he had ever done to punish her. That didn't really call for loathing, did it?

"You go first!" Milly secured her stocking rope to the window and grabbed my waist, propelling me forward.

"But Milly—"

"Go!"

"I won't! You go first!"

I couldn't see Milly's eyes, but I knew there was a wild anger flooding them. Obediently she yanked up her checkered skirts and swung her leg out of the window, holding firmly onto the rope. Then she skillfully climbed down it. I watched her with mortification, my stomach lurching when I saw the distance she had to cover to reach solid ground. I would surely die. There was no hope for me.

But I had to try. All I could see below me was smoke. There was no ground as far as I could see, only a sea of black and gray. I didn't even know if Milly had made it down all right. Hanging on a hope of thread as thin as the tip of a needle, I grabbed the rope like my life depended on it. And it did. Slowly, apprehensively, I shimmied my body down the rope. Ounces of oxygen filled my lungs at a time, and as a result, tingling sensations assaulted my legs and arms and fingertips, letting me know I had a short time left before I would faint. At some point I lost all sense of everything, and dark fuzz invaded my mind. I fell into a deep black sea, a window of my imagination. I fainted. Not able to hold on anymore, I let go of the rope. After that, I lost control and insight of everything.

~

A cold splash of water awoke me, and sweet, fresh oxygen filled my body. Many faces stood over me, voices echoed through the air. I opened my eyes and saw Milly's face. She let out a cry of relief and swung me into her arms.

"Where's Papa?" I demanded, but as I looked around at the scene before me, I saw no white faces, only black ones. I sat on a green patch of grass a distance from my house, although I could see the scene perfectly. Negroes furiously scrambled to and fro with hopeless buckets of water, fighting the persisting red flames that flew from the windows. I watched in horror as the fractious blazes crept up to the third story, smoke floating out from my window. No one dared go back inside. A wagon pulled by furiously galloping horses stopped to let its passengers jump out. Firemen scrambled around, aiding the slaves in efforts to put out the flames. I watched in absolute mortification and horror as my house crumbled into ashes. The efforts to put out the flames were hopeless. The house was destroyed, and there was nothing a little water could do about it. *Life goes on . . . life goes on . . .*

"Your Papa'll be fine, honey. He'll get out of there. You'll see." Milly soothed, stroking my hair. But I didn't believe her. It was too late. Papa was trapped in his room, and he wouldn't even try to get out. Of course he wouldn't. He didn't care about living anymore. Not since Mother died. Ever since that ill-fated day, all life had been drained from his body. I could picture perfectly his swollen red face, due to his endless tears and limitless bottles of whiskey. He'd taken up the drink and had become addicted ten years ago, when Mother had perished. I was only seven then, and much too young to understand what it was that made my dear papa so sad. Papa had always been so happy and kind to me. He used to kiss my cheek and hug me and speak to me softly, just like Milly was doing now. I used to snuggle up to him when I was smaller and throw my arms around his neck, gazing up into his handsome face. I could still smell his scent of pipe smoke and fresh peppermint, still see his smiling green eyes and brown beard, still hear his low, husky voice and feel his warm breath tickle my ear when he whispered into it. I loved Papa always, even though he didn't show his love for me anymore. He would get up in the mornings, eat his meals without a word, then escape to his office for the day and drink until the pain was numb. Lately it had gotten worse, since my mother's birthday just passed not a week ago. Nowadays Papa never even looked at me. Apparently I was blossoming to look just like she had, and Papa couldn't bear it. No matter what I said or did, things just got worse for Papa. He was slowly killing himself, and all I could do was stand by and watch. And all because of Mother. The woman who I'd never really known.

She had been a different person. She'd never told me she loved me, and I would rarely receive attention or affection from her. I don't even remember what an embrace from her felt like, it happened so seldom. Mother was too caught up in her social life to pay me any mind. She always wore the most fashionable gowns and the tightest corsets, adorning herself in precious jewelry and extravagant diamonds. She always threw parties and flounced around the neighborhood in her carriage, calling on friends and attending social meetings of all kinds. The only thing Mother cared about was money and Papa. She loved Papa. I don't know why she didn't love me, but she truly cared with her whole heart for him. Her face always brightened to the deep sound of his voice and the sight of his smiling face. And Papa loved her in return. He always told me I was the reason he lived, the apple of his eye, and that he loved me more than anything in the whole world. Sometimes I wonder if he had told Mother the same things.

Mother had been very beautiful. Everyone said I was the perfect image of her, with white porcelain skin and honey-strawberry curls. We both had petite statures, with high cheek bones and fragile features. Except while Mother had eyes the color of a sunny, blue sky, mine were dark green, like emeralds. Even though we looked alike, Mother and I were worlds apart. I never once cared about parties or jewels or dresses, and I never took notice of my looks. I loved the outdoors, loved the swift breeze that rustled the leaves and the thick, lush grass that curled around my feet. I adored the birds' happy songs and the sunny blue sky. But of course, proper young ladies *never* played outside, in hopes to preserve their dainty, white complexions. The only times I'd been allowed outside to play were when I was very small, and even then I was forced to wear a bonnet.

After a while, I got used to the fact that I had to be proper and somber, that fun was not allowed. At least, not for me. The other girls in class seemed to get along well enough in their lessons of Conversational French and needlepoint, among others. I'd attended Miss Mortemeyer's Academy for Young Ladies for six years, learning such things as how to behave at the dinner table and when to serve tea, along with arithmetic, literature, music, French, science, and history. In all honesty, the only class I'd really paid attention to, the one I absolutely adored, was art. I loved the idea of taking a white canvas, open to the word, and spilling the colors of my heart out onto it. After I'd learned I had a great aptitude for creating artwork, winning first prize in the Academy's watercolors contest, I budged Papa to buy me paints and a sketchpad to practice my newfound talent. I would go outside and sit in the shade of our giant tree and paint different landscapes I saw or birds that sat perched on a branch. Sometimes I would pick up a pencil and sketch scenes, adding colors later. The first portrait I did was of Milly. Milly, my chambermaid, was only about five years my senior. She took care of me and gave me the attention and love I lacked from my mother.

One day I told Milly to sit in the rocking chair by the window, the one that she always sat in to read me stories or sing soft hymns to me before bed. I set the crocheting materials in her lap and posed her just so, then picked up my pencil and began to draw. I was only about twelve, but my picture was surprisingly praiseworthy. I made her big eyes just perfect, adding the spark that was usually found in their chocolaty depths. I gave just the right amount of shading to her ebony skin and finished the picture off with the sweet outline of her full lips.

Milly was the most beautiful Negro I had ever seen in my whole life. She was slender and medium-framed, yet tough and strong. I adored her, loving her the way a daughter should love her mother. She and our head cook, who I always referred to as plain old "Cook", taught me the ways of Jesus, that He wasn't just a man that lived in church. I put my faith in Him after Milly assured me He was indeed everything you needed to live. Milly told me He loved us all more than anyone on earth ever could. Of course I attended church with my parents on Sunday mornings, but Mother and Papa never talked to me about God or practiced bible verses with me outside of church. After a while I realized my parents only attended church because society expected them to. It was no more than a mere obligation on my Mother's part. Milly and Cook helped me understand the ways of Jesus better, teaching me songs and bible verses about Him. They told me when you have no one else to turn to, God will be there for you. And I believed it.

Sometimes I heard Milly talking to other slaves about freedom. Only when I got older did I realize how badly the slaves wanted to be free. They wanted freedom almost as much as they wanted air to breathe. They would get up early in the mornings and congregate in the fields, picking the cotton and preparing it for Papa to sell. I know because sometimes I watched them from my bedroom window. One summer morning I purposely woke up at five so I could see them walk down to the fields from their tiny wooden cabins. I found that they get their start early, when the sun is still a heavy golden ball peeking over the horizon. They begin to spread out on the fields, gradually, ghost-like. Black men, women, and even children bustle through the endless rows of white cotton, bending over at each plant and yanking. Angry sores swell and redden on their fingers and callused hands, due to the thorny sheaths on the bottoms of the tufts. Under the fiery, hot sun, the slaves work until dusk, all the while singing low, haunting hymns, ones I thought were absolutely beautiful. Like nothing I've ever heard before. I asked Papa what he thought about the music the slaves make together, and he called it "horrid screeching". I asked Milly once if that's what she thought of the slaves' singing.

"Honey, those songs them men and women are singin' come deep from the soul. They ain't screeching at all."

At first, the singing scared me. It reminded me of sad, distant things I could not quite place my finger on. But after a while, I got used to it, and I even memorized some of the words. I enjoyed their songs and thought their rich, full voices were the most beautiful things on the face of the earth. One song in particular stayed with me, like a ghost. I hummed it to Gordon, our stable master, one day while

I was down visiting him and the horses, and he told me it was called, "Go Down, Moses".

"Now, Missy, don't be singin' them songs." he scolded. "They ain't what propa lil' ladies should be singin.'"

But I couldn't resist humming it, and I pleaded with him to at least tell me the words. When he refused to compromise with me, I'd skipped up to the kitchen and asked Cook about it. After some begging, she finally gave in and sang it for me. I quickly fetched a pencil and paper and scribbled down the words, listening carefully to the beautiful huskiness of Cook's singing voice.

"When Israel was in Egypt's land,
    Let my people go;
Oppressed so hard they could not stand,
    Let my people go;"

And when it came time for the chorus, I could sing along since I already knew it.

"Go down, Moses, way down
    in Egypt's land;
Tell old Pharaoh, to let my people go."

~

"Missy. Missy Catherine." The housemaid, Aggie, brought me back down to earth, shaking me from my thoughts. Her ample body swayed as she planted herself in front of me, making me look into her black eyes. They were filled with worry and care. "Your daddy . . . he ain't . . . he . . ."

I shook my head, silencing her. I already knew what she was going to say. Strangely, it didn't bother me as much as I thought it would. Maybe because I knew all along Papa was going to die. Except I always imagined I would find him dead in his sleep, drowned in his excessive drinking. Well, what did it matter? Papa hadn't loved me anymore anyway.

He had abandoned me when I was growing up, the time I needed him most. For all I knew, he had died a long time ago, when Mother did. His soul had slipped away, leaving only a careless shell in its place.

Then a dawning horror struck me like an unexpected bolt of lightning. Where would I go? I had no grandparents, no aunts or uncles, no family at all. What would I do with the plantation? The house?

"When you have no one, turn to Massa Jesus," Milly had once advised in one of our unofficial sermons.

What could Jesus possibly have to do with *this* situation? Unless he could magically summon me a new house and bring Papa back, I was out of luck. As I watched the last flames burn out, leaving only a dusty, gray shell that used to be my home, I realized my life was as destructed as the remains of my house. My home was gone, as well as my parents, and nothing could change that.

Black faces huddled around me, some filled with tears and despair, others with expressions of surprise. I could feel their questions bore into me. *Where will we go? What will become of us?* Honestly, I had no idea. Wherever I went, I couldn't drag along all these slaves with me. Who would I stay with? I tried to think logically. Papa surely had a plan for me in outlined in his will. Yes, that was it. The will. I had to see his will before anything.

A flood of sudden emotions rushed through me. I collapsed onto the ground, letting my tears escape from my eyes. I knew it would displease Papa if I cried, for he had always been strictly against tears. He believed that if a person cried, it was a sign of weakness. I came to realize that was partially why he sheltered himself. He was ashamed of the tears that fell so fluently from his eyes.

As if Milly and I were the same person, she toppled over next to me and started whimpering, too. I am uncertain of how long we lay there, Milly humming a soft hymn to herself, the heat of our bodies pressed against one another. I remained sprawled out on the ground, slowly letting out all my feelings, one tear at a time. After some time, what seemed like hours, I sat up and wiped away my sobs. Composing myself, I rose to my feet, shaking off the dust from my night dress.

"Gordon!" I called out for my faithful stable master. He rushed over to me, looking down into my eyes with distress in his own. "Hitch up the carriage. I'd like to go to the attorney's office."

"Yes, Missy." Gordon hurried off to the stables. I took one last look at the house. The firemen stood around, conversing with the slaves. They poured water out of buckets feebly now, the flames almost dead and the smoke beginning to settle. Milly and I were alone now, standing together and letting our eyes survey everything which was home and which was ruined. I directed my attention back to Gordon, watching him select two of the calmer horses, Patches and Luna, harnessing them to the buggy. The barn had not been touched, nor the slaves houses on the outskirts of the fields. Only the house had been wrecked in the fire.

When Gordon stood with the carriage in front of me, I gathered up my night dress skirts and climbed into the carriage.

I looked back to Milly, her arms crossed tightly and her face solemn and cold.

"I'll be right back. Stay here." I spoke softly to her, then nodded towards Gordon, giving him permission to go. As I was led down the cobblestones, the horses' hooves clicking softly on the ground, I thought to myself. What was I to do?

Pray.

I shuddered at what the air seemed to whisper. Pray? Not now. Now I had to worry about where I was going to go. I needed to find out what my father left for me, if anything. I needed to know what he intended to do with the plantation. And I didn't need to know about praying. Those words Milly taught me that I mindlessly put every ounce of my faith into weren't meant for me anymore. They just weren't true. No god would hurt a person so much, treat them like such rubbish as I had been treated. Such ill fate I had been through and still no answer from God. I was disgusted with Him and I wouldn't pray. I couldn't.

Shutting my eyes, I rested my head upon the seat. In a flash of alarm, my eyes opened again. I suddenly remembered my appearance. A night gown. I let out a foreign bark of a laugh.

"What's funny, Missy?" Gordon asked, gaze firmly fixed on the road.

"How am I supposed to waltz in the bank looking like this? I look a fright."

"When you wake up and there's a fire in your house, it ain't matterin' what you look like, just so's your safe," he replied.

Gordon made sense. He was wise for his age. I figured him to be not a day over forty-five. A little bit of white dotted his beard and streaked the hair on his temple, but his face was still black and smooth, like the ebony keys on a piano.

"You're right." But I felt a little embarrassed. My night dress reached my ankles, but was made of such a flimsy material I bet a person could see right through me.

Inside the office, I sighed with relief as I saw no one in the little business but an elderly man at the counter. It was Mr. Smittle, our family's lawyer—or rather, my lawyer. He and Papa were friends from way back. He was kind-looking, with gray hair and mild eyes that assured understanding. I could see the evident surprise on his face as he glanced up at me. I felt my cheeks burn, but I confidently strode up to the table and stated my case.

"Miss Carey?" He stood up from his busy place at his desk. "Are you hurt? What has happened?

"There was a fire this morning. My home is ruined. And my father is . . ."

"Oh, my dear . . ." I saw he was completely devastated and didn't know what to say. "I'm so very sorry. Are you hurt? Do you need anything—"

"I am fine. What I would like to see is my father's will, please. I have nowhere to go and no one to go to. I need to see what my father's plans for me were."

He nodded and then descended into a smaller room at the south side of the building. I heard the rustle of papers and the opening and closing of drawers, and then Mr. Smittle emerged back, an envelope cradled in both hands.

"This is it, Miss Carey."

I took the envelope from him and opened it, quickly perusing the document inside. What Papa said in his will surprised me. He had hundreds of thousands of dollars in the bank, and it was all willed to me! And the plantation was mine, as well as the slaves. A pang of dread shot through me. I couldn't possibly manage it on my own.

"Where are you going to go?"

I swallowed a lump in my throat and bit my lip, looking up from the will into concerned eyes.

"I inherit the whole plantation. I suppose I knew that part from the start. But I cannot keep it. I have to sell it. The only relatives I have left are my godparents. I forget where they live . . ."

I read further into the will. At last I found them. I read aloud: "If my daughter is not of age to keep the inheritance, she shall be put under the care of Mr. and Mrs. Walter of Saint Louis, Missouri, her godparents".

Missouri? No. No. No. No.

"Thank you Mr. Smittle."

I strode out of the office before he could utter a single word.

"Any luck, Missy?" Gordon asked as I slid into the carriage.

"Would you please take me to the train station now?"

I'm sure I sounded cross, but I really didn't care. I massaged my throbbing temple, all kinds of ideas and questions zooming through my mind, mocking me. Well, I knew one thing for sure. I would free the slaves. I wouldn't have them accompany me to Saint Louis, and I also would not have them sold to God knows where. The sudden jolt of the carriage demolished my thoughts. Gordon helped me out of the seat, and I quickly walked up to the ticket stand, aware of several disapproving pairs of eyes settling upon on me and my night gown.

"I'd like to know when the next train to St. Louis leaves," I stated with as much dignity as I could muster when I reached the box office.

A blond boy of about my age looked up at me, glancing at my figure evident through the flimsy gown. When he looked back into my eyes, I could see the reddening of his cheeks. I didn't have time to explain or to worry about my appearance.

"Four, tomorrow, miss," he managed to say sheepishly.

I handed him the money for the desired price, then took my ticket and hurried away to the carriage. An elderly lady glued to a man's arm looked me up and down with disgust. If only she knew who I was. Why, Papa was the wealthiest man in Charleston! Or, at least, he had been. I pressed my lips together in a tight, hard line, looking Gordon in the eyes.

"Where to now, Missy?" he asked with an encouraging wink.

"The bank." I didn't know how I was going to pull this off, but I had to. I simply had to.

When I stepped inside, Mr. Morgen, the banker, rushed to my side. He had also been one of Papa's trusted, old friends.

"I heard the news, Miss Carey. A fireman just stopped in to tell us. Is your father really . . . ?"

I nodded, my eyes flooding with tears once again. Promptly, I presented the will to him, as no words were necessary. He knew why I was there. After leading me to my safe, Mr. Morgen, the banker, unlocked it, and inside, hidden treasures of my family's past were so carefully stored. I recognized some of the objects, one being my mother's old hair comb adorned with pearls and rubies. There was also an emerald necklace and a tiny wooden music box. Mr. Morgen pulled bundles of paper money out of the safe as well.

"You're not old enough to take this yet, Miss Carey. Just come back when you're eighteen and we will have everything safe for you."

"Yes, sir," I told him. Then I thanked him politely and carefully walked back to the carriage.

"Let's go home now, please, Gordon," I breathed, offering a weak smile.

"Yes, Missy," he replied before giving the reins a switch.

As we neared upon the house, now just shelled remains and sooty ashes, I let out a sigh. An official stood in the yard, questioning Milly and Cook. Milly stood there with a grave face while Cook did all the speaking. The other slaves stood in groups, talking and weeping, and I even saw some men filing through the rubbish, bending over ever so often to scoop up a broken photo frame or a porcelain dish tainted black. I couldn't even make out where Father's room had been; the house was so misshapen. I wondered if there really was anything left of him. Tears stung my eyes, and my throat burned. I wondered what the slaves had found left of him. But I didn't want to know, after all.

I couldn't understand why God had done this. First He took away my mother, then my father and my home. What more could He possibly want from me? Was He just trying to hurt me, to make me die inside? I choked back the persisting tears that I promised would never come again. Milly took me in her arms again as soon as I emerged from the carriage. How could I possibly say goodbye to her? I loved her like a mother. In all ways except one, she *was* my mother. She had taken care of me, soothed me, and had served in the place of my mother, giving me the love I never received.

"Milly," I whispered.

"Yes, baby?" she said into my hair.

"I can't stay here and run this plantation. I'm only seventeen. I'm going to go live with my godparents in Missouri. They are the only ones I have left. And I don't even know them . . . But nevertheless, you are a free woman. Everyone is free to go."

Her breathing stopped, and she loosened her grip on my shoulders, pulling back to look at me dead in the eyes. Her face, streamed with tears, took on a new emotion.

"You're free. Just like you always wanted." I fought back the tears that just wouldn't stop bothering me. All the slaves gathered around me, and I turned to them, forcing a smile to my lips.

~

It seemed to me that Time went by at its own pace. In the darkest times, it went by so slow you could swear it wasn't at all moving. In times of happiness, Time zoomed by, like a horse running at a full gallop. The day my whole world crumbled down, Time decided to trick me and go as fast as it possibly could. I barely had enough time to take a breath the rest of the day and the next, having a proper, little ceremony for Papa, hurrying to the courthouse to sign papers for the slaves' freedom, saying goodbye to Milly and the others, picking through the ashes for anything left, collecting a large sum of money from the bank, purchasing a new wardrobe, toiletries, and a proper traveler's suitcase, telegramming the Walters so they'd meet me at the train station, and getting it all done before nightfall.

Saying goodbye to Milly was the hardest thing I ever had to do. We embraced each other for what seemed like hours, a bundle of emotions coursing through us both. No words were spoken, except when I told her I loved her, and she smiled back, unable to speak. The tears in her eyes and the expression on her face held more words for me than an entire speech would. Gordon was the second hardest goodbye, since I cared deeply for him as well. His big, strong arms wrapped around me, enveloping me in a warm embrace. I knew I would never see any of my slave friends again, and the thought killed me inside.

When I boarded the train, Time settled down like a horse coming to a trot. I sat by myself in one of the seats, preparing myself for the long trip ahead. The night before I'd stayed with Mr. Smittle and his wife, as they were kind enough to offer me the guest room and hot meals. Even though their home was beautifully furnished, it offered me no comfort. Sleep had evaded me, as I could not keep from worrying and crying about Papa and my house and all the change about to come.

On the train ride my mind was restless while my body starved for sleep. Once or twice I would doze off, but the lady beside me would start to snore and I'd be wide awake again. My head reeled as I gazed out the window the entire ride, letting my eyes shut if I could ease my mind enough to do so. It was the most merciless and formidable train ride I had ever endured in my seventeen years.

When we finally arrived in St. Louis, my stomach churned. My head was as heavy as ever, and I felt disgusted with myself. I longed for a hot bath to help cleanse my mind, as well as my body. Instead, I forced myself forward, stepping out from the train. The busy sights before my eyes made my heart thump with acceleration. Missouri wasn't as different as I had expected. Of course, there was no beautiful ocean or sparkling harbor like there was in Charleston. But a wide, glimmering river winded through the city, and that was sufficient. Thousands of trees covered the enormous hills of the countryside, buildings dotted the cities, and people flocked like pigeons on the sidewalks. After my feet touched the solid ground, I made my way through the mess of noisy people and searched frantically for a sign with my name on it. Not a one. I frantically looked about me, slithering through the crowd. No one even looked at me. After waiting and searching for a while, I finally gave up. Hadn't they received my telegram? Perhaps I could find a person that would tell me where the Walters lived. I walked along the busy cobblestone streets, a cool breeze rushing through my loosely pinned hair, until I reached the bank. There, I put on my best smile and marched up to the desk.

"Excuse me, sir," I said to the man seated behind a desk. After he glanced up, I continued. "This may be a silly question, but—"

"There is no such thing," he brushed off my comment with a flick of his hand and looked me sternly in the eye.

"Oh, well, do you know of a man named Andrew Walter?"

"Yes, yes." He folded his round, plump hands on the table, regarding momentarily his pocket watch set out on the desk. "Mr. Walter. Of course."

"Well, can you please tell me where he lives? I'm his goddaughter."

Grabbing a clean sheet of paper, he scribbled down some sloppy words and impulsively thrust it at me, once again staring with consternation at the papers that were cluttered on his desk.

"Thank you," I offered politely, and he merely nodded. Pleasant man.

As I pushed open the wide wooden door of the bank, I tried to make out the words so carelessly written on the paper. 166 Abe's Avenue. Oh, now didn't that solve everything? Gathering up my skirts, I stopped the first carriage that hobbled down the street.

"Yes, miss?" the buggy's driver yelled out to me. He was a black man, and the whites of his eyes glistened ivory against his dark, coal-black irises.

"I was wondering if you could be so kind as to tell me where Abe's Avenue is," I called back.

"Actually, we're on our way there," a woman called from inside the carriage. "Climb aboard."

I smiled in relief and stepped onto the street. The buggy's driver helped me in with my suitcase, and I silently nestled in next to the seat by the window.

"What's your name, darlin'?" the woman asked. The smiling eyes that met mine revealed a heart of the utmost of kindnesses. She was a large woman, wide and seemingly strong, yet graceful. The graying hair piled on top of her head was set above a smiling face with faded blue eyes. She was about thirty years my senior, I assumed.

"Catherine," I replied quietly.

There was a man seated across from us, and I supposed he was her husband. His cheery eyes met mine, and I looked away shyly. He possessed a tall, thin frame and a balding head of dark hair streaked with gray. He, too, had the gentlest eyes, though.

"Well, what's bringing you to Abe's Avenue?" the man asked with a wink.

I smiled. "I have family that live there." There was no need to go into any details.

"I see. What address do they live at? There's only a few houses on that street."

I peered at the paper. "166."

The man and woman exchanged shocked glances.

"Did you say 166?" A grin formed on the woman's face.

"Yes, ma'am," I replied, shoving a blonde curl behind my ear.

"Well, then you're in good luck, darlin'. 'Cause that's exactly where we're headed."

"You're friends of the Walters?" I was surprised.

"Well, not exactly," the man said with a hint of amusement in his eyes.

"We *are* the Walters, darlin'," the woman said.

"You're Andrew Walter?" I asked the man seated across from me.

He nodded. "That I am. That I am."

"Saints be! I'm Catherine Carey. Your godchild."

Mrs. Walter gasped, and a hand fluttered to her breast. Her husband's jaw dropped several inches, and his brows quirked together.

"But . . . how'd you get here? And where is your father?" Mrs. Walter asked.

I didn't know how to tell them this. They hadn't received my telegram after all. I had much explaining to do. And would they believe me? After a moment of hesitation, I offered a short explanation, as I was weary of the sadness of the story and felt it unnecessary to tell.

"I took a train," I smiled. "And I sent a telegram. You must not have received it. But I had explained my reason for coming in it. And . . ."

I could tell by their faces that they were indeed puzzled. They wanted to know everything.

Mrs. Walter placed a comforting hand over mine. "What is it dear?"

"There was a fire yesterday in the morning. I don't know how it was instigated, but it succeeded in burning down my entire house. And my father could not escape in time. He perished within the house." The words sounded so foreign, so strange. It was as if they didn't seem right leaving my lips.

"Oh, heavens, no . . ." Mrs. Walter trailed off, a distant look in her eyes. She placed a hand over her mouth. Mr.

Walter stared at me for a moment before covering his face with his hands and rubbing his temples.

The hushed perplexity was so intense that I grew uncomfortably hot. My corset suddenly felt too tight, and I could barely breathe. Warm tears remained unshed in my eyes, and I brushed them away with my hair, looking out the window for a distraction.

A hand covering mine brought my attention back to Mrs. Walter.

"I have no other family either. So I thought I might stay with your family for a while," I explained carefully, "until I can perhaps find my own place to live."

"Of course you are welcome to come live with us."

"Thank you." I looked down at my boots. "I was unsure about what to do. My father instructed me to come to you in his will."

"Yes, of course," Mrs. Walter soothed, releasing my hand. To the driver, she shouted, "Just keep on going, to our house."

The rest of the ride to the house was quiet, except for the occasional sneeze or sigh. We rode along a vast outer dirt road, much different than I'd expected. It was rather deserted, with no wagons or people in sight. I could tell we were in the country part of town. Only grass and trees stretched for miles and miles. Below us, tall stalks of corn were neatly planted. A few minutes later, the stalks of corn turned into rows of tomatoes and lettuce, radishes and carrots and even potatoes. My stomach growled, reminding me I had not eaten in a day and a half, as my stomach had rejected the thought of food.

Cows grazed lazily in a huge pasture abundant with little white flowers and golden dandelions. Along with cows and chickens I saw horses, their long, gentle faces sticking out of the stables in curiosity at the sound of our approaching buggy. A stable and a barn stood on the outskirts of the grassy fields, near an old farmhouse, which I presumed to be the Walters' home.

The old house was badly in need of a fresh, new coat of paint. It was a two-story, while my mansion had been three. An outhouse sat to the east of the house in the backyard. A huge porch circled around the entire house, and a wooden swing hung from a nearby branch. I counted six windows on the front of the house, four being on the top level. The front door was the only thing that appeared new. It was bright blue, and had obviously just been painted. Several rickety wooden steps led up to the porch. The entire house itself was set on flat ground nearly fifty feet from the road, surrounded by emerald grass and backed by hills lavishly abundant with forests and other wild flora.

"That's our place," Mrs. Walter whispered.

So if these people would take me, this would be my house. My *home.* I couldn't tell what came to me more as a surprise, the fact that I was in Missouri on a farm, or the realization that I hadn't any parents or real place to call my own. I was an orphan. My throat went dry, and I could only nod in reply. The Negro driver jumped down from the buggy seat, scooping up a little black girl who waddled out to meet him, ragged doll in hand.

"Thank you for driving us, Nathaniel. It was very kind of you," Mrs. Walter smiled brightly. I wondered why Mrs. Walter thanked her slave in such a manner. As if she was in debt to him for his service. We never did so.

"You think the baby is still asleep?" Mr. Walter asked.

The man drew his attention back to him. "I wouldn't doubt it. Our baby boy sleeps most of his life so far. And Nina's prob'ly still restin' too."

"Nathaniel, this is our goddaughter, Catherine Carey," Mrs. Walter gestured proudly to me. "We didn't even know it until she told us who she was. We haven't seen her since she was a tiny thing."

"Pleased to meet you," Nathaniel smiled, holding out his hand for me to shake. I took it hesitantly but pulled away fast.

"Come on, dear, let's us go on inside," Mrs. Walter offered gently, guiding me towards the door. Nathaniel and Mr. Walter stayed behind and conversed, no doubt discussing the odd situation involving me.

Mrs. Walter and I soundly made our way up the old, white stairs to the front door. The slave, Nathaniel, reminded me so much of Jack, Milly's secret beau. Jack was a slave of the neighbors' back home. I wasn't supposed to find out about him, but one evening, as we had company over, I discovered their secret affair. The adults chattered around the dining table and I sat obediently, hushed and jaded. I needed Milly at that moment, so I excused myself and skipped off to find her. She hadn't been sitting around chatting with the slaves in the kitchen, where I'd left her, so I went all about the house trying to scavenge her out, running up and down the staircases and sashaying about the halls in my flouncy dinner dress and satin slippers. I thought to look outside, so I stepped out onto the balcony. It overlooked the plantation and the elegant rose garden beneath. Suddenly I heard soft laughter ripple from the garden below me. There, just on the bench shaded by a giant tree, sat Milly with Jack. He was gently whispering in her ear, making her whole face sparkle, a perfect bright smile evident in the dark night. I had never seen her so beautiful. Although that evening while she laced my corset and helped me dress, she had unusually taken the extra time to fix up her own hair and scrub her face. I even peeked back into my room to see her dab my rouge onto her lips and cheeks. She must have known Jack would have been there.

I gasped when I saw Jack bend down to steal a kiss from Milly's soft, dark mouth. She kissed him back, then whispered something to him before flitting away. My Milly was in love with Jack. And, sadly, it was forbidden. I had overheard Cook tell Milly the next day about how love and slaves didn't mix. I heard her say that slaves had too much weight on their shoulders to get caught up in a love affair, that love brought nothing but trouble and tears. I pitied Milly, but never once told her I knew. It was her business, not mine. And, oh, how I wished someone would whisper in my ear like that, kiss me tenderly and make my face glow like Milly's that night. But of course, I was only thirteen at the time, and much too young for a suitor or a kiss.

Inside, the big farmhouse was old-fashioned and worn, yet I felt a sense of peace the second I stepped across the threshold. It felt comfortable and homey, like what a true home was supposed to feel like. The faded blue wallpaper glued to the walls was completely covered with knickknacks and photos and paintings. Wooden floors covered the entire foyer, and the house emanated the scent of soap and fresh linen. A mahogany staircase was to the left of the foyer, leading to the bedrooms upstairs, I supposed. The walls above the stairs, along with all the other walls I could see, were abundant with clocks: big clocks, little clocks, wooden clocks, grandfather clocks, and coo-coo clocks, among other kinds of clocks, dotted the walls and lined the furniture. Listening carefully to the rhythms and looking at a few of the long minute hands, I realized that each one ticked on a different schedule. I suppressed a chuckle at this.

I knew that at one time the house had been a dream. If only someone would swish a coat of paint on the outside and take down the wall paper, making a few little repairs here and there, the house would sparkle just like new. In spite of its cluttered condition, the house seemed very clean.

"Dear, let me show you your room," Mrs. Walter smiled, taking my slender hand in her chubby one. "Come along, up the stairs we go!"

"Mrs. Walter, I know this is such short notice, and I know you probably don't wish me to be here. I promise to be grateful and I will help—." The words tumbled out of my mouth awkwardly, and she waved her hand to hush me.

"I intend to take good care of you. You're my goddaughter, after all. I know you've only seen me once, and you were a tiny thing, but I plan to make you at home here."

She led me to the guest room. "You'll bring new life to this house. Sometimes, me and Jonathon and my husband get so lonely. Why, Johnny spends most of his time outdoors! He only comes in for eatin' and sleepin'!"

Letting out a chuckle, Mrs. Walter plopped down on the bed.

"Who's Jonathon?" I inquired.

"Oh, why, he's my son. You've seen him too, but I wouldn't expect you to remember. Wait, let me guess how old you are now." She tapped her index finger on her chin, staring upward, mumbling a math problem under her breath. "Sixteen?"

"Close, but no. I am seventeen."

"Ah. Time flies." Mrs. Walter stood, hands on her hips. "Well, I'll leave you to your room. Go ahead and unpack your things. You can join us for supper in about an hour."

Then, she placed a motherly hand on my shoulder. "And if you need anything, tell me. You have some things in your suitcase I guess?"

"Yes, some things that I purchased back home before I came. I shouldn't need anything yet. But if I think of something I will let you know."

"That sounds all right to me," she smiled before she was off, her silent footsteps carrying her out of the room.

I looked about me, pleased at what I saw. A small bed dressed in a crimson and royal blue quilt was placed in the corner of the room, and by it sat a wooden nightstand. A dresser and a mirror were near the front of the room, the latter covered with white, lacy doilies and clocks. I counted five clocks in the room altogether. In spite of myself, I giggled softly. One of Mrs. Walter's fancies, I supposed.

When I was smaller, I would have loved the idea of living in the countryside, glad to be rid of corsets and gowns and hoop skirts. Over the years, though, I had become accustomed to them. Certainly Mrs. Walter didn't wear a corset or a hoop skirt. I would need to purchase more practical clothes, and when I did, they would not be anything like I used to wear. I smiled at the thought. Finally, something to look forward to.

Just then, I heard a soft neighing sound coming from the stables beneath the open window. Carefully peeling back the curtain, I saw a finely built young man guide a black horse through the stable. Jonathon? I placed the curtain back to the way it was. Soon, however, I returned to the window, curiosity edging me to look out upon him once more so I might glimpse his face.

He wore a white linen shirt with the sleeves rolled up to his elbows, revealing strong, brown forearms. His hair fell in dark waves. I watched, intrigued, as he swung his leg around the horse, settling himself on the saddle. He whispered something to it, clicked his tongue, and slowly the horse trotted away into the grassy green fields. I envied his freedom, the way he could saddle his horse any old time and ride out like there was nothing to life at all. I sighed and moved away from the window.

For dinner, I was summoned by a holler from Mrs. Walter that rang clear through the house. I didn't want to go to dinner. I wanted to lay down on the bed and just rest and think. My appetite was entirely gone, as my nerves were up, and even though I knew my stomach beckoned for food, I felt as if I would not be able to eat. I just wanted to be alone. Arguing with myself inwardly, I stared into the mirror at my pale face. I traced the dark circles that hung beneath my eyes. I looked awful. How long had it been since I had seen my reflection? Disgusted, I looked away.

Reluctantly deciding to eat with the others, I pinched my cheeks to force some color into my face, then took the ivory-handled brush and passed it through my unruly hair several times before arranging it in pins. Despite the bruised lines beneath my tired eyes, I suppose I was pretty enough, naturally. My nose was round and small, and my eyes were wide almond shapes, soft and green. My hair fell in dark golden ripples around my face, cascading down beneath my shoulders in glossy curls. It behaved when it wanted to. It rarely wanted to. Taking one last wistful side glance in the mirror, I inhaled deeply and descended down the staircase, feeling one step short of confident.

When I entered the dining room, I was surprised to find it empty, except for the clocks and furniture, of course.

"In here, darlin'," Mrs. Walter called from the kitchen. I hurried in, wondering why they ate their meals in the kitchen. Papa and I had always dined in the spacious dining hall, adorned with jeweled chandeliers and imported furniture made with rich mahogany. The kitchen was absolutely no comparison. The clocks ticked out my heartbeat as I took the remaining wobbly chair. I didn't make eye contact with anyone, as I could feel the flaming heat rise to my face.

"Sorry," I whispered to Mrs. Walter as I spread a cloth napkin across my lap.

"Don't worry, darlin'. Now, let's say grace," she said, taking her husband's hand. Next she took mine, and I nearly jumped out of my seat. It had been so long since I'd prayed at meal time, I almost forgot how. Papa had always just dug in as soon as courses were served.

And that's when Jonathon's pale blue eyes met mine. I realized the expectant look on his face meant that I had to offer my hand in order to complete the circle. Awkwardly I slid it across the table, linking hands with his. His warm palm covered mine, absorbed mine almost. Heat spread through me, into my face and down my neck. I blushed with embarrassment, praying that the humiliation would soon be over and I could leave the room.

"Heavenly Father, we thank You for this meal You so graciously provided for us. We thank You for Catherine; please let her be comfortable here and make this her home. We know that with Your tender hand upon her, grief will be forgotten and she will be able to continue on with a happy life. Bless all of us here, and bless the food, so it will nourish and strengthen our bodies. Amen."

Jonathon released my hand quickly, and I bit my bottom lip so hard I could taste a drop of blood. Even though my stomach begged for food, I couldn't eat a single bite. Not wanting to seem rude, I pretended to take tiny tastes, moving my fork around on the plate. I felt so uncomfortable at the table, although there really was no reason to be. It seemed as if the Walters were quite relaxed in my presence, however, staring at their plates as they shoveled forkful after forkful of the meat and potatoes into their mouths.

"Jonathon." Mrs. Walter's eyes bore into his. "Don't you have anything to say to Catherine?" To me she whispered, "He knows about everything, darlin'. We thought it best to tell him."

His mind seemed to be elsewhere, for his gaze was fixated on the gravy dish, his fingers cupping his chin and his brows furrowing in deep thought. He had eaten incredibly fast, his plate completely bare. He glanced up involuntarily at the sound of his name being called.

"What? Oh." His gaze met and locked on mine. He searched my face, as if contemplating me. Finally he breathed and said, "Nice to meet you. And I'm sorry to hear about . . . everything. Good dinner, Mama." And with that, he pushed back his chair, leaving the table in a swift pace.

Mrs. Walter shook her head when she heard the door slam. "Excuse his behavior, darlin'. He's not used to havin' pretty girls in the house."

"Just shy, is all," Mr. Walter added, smiling at me.

I nodded, though I didn't fully understand. He didn't seem shy. He seemed rude. Sorry to hear about . . . everything? Mrs. Walter needn't have said anything to him in the first place. I certainly did not need his false pity.

After dinner, I watched as Mrs. Walter cleaned up the dishes. Where was the slave maid? So as not to be rude, I cleared away plates as well, joining her in the kitchen afterwards to wash them. There wasn't a slave in sight. Strange.

"Catherine?" Mrs. Walter called my name from her place in front of the sink.

"Yes?"

"Things are probably a lot different here, aren't they?"

"Yes," I mused, "a little."

"Well, I know you had slaves, didn't you?"

Where was this going? "Yes."

"Here, we don't. We have laborers to help with the farm. We give them fair pay in return. If they don't like it here, then they can quit. But they do like it here."

I gulped. Paid Negroes? I had never heard of such a thing. "I understand."

"Well, I just didn't want you to think I was crazy, 'cause I'm doin' the dishes," she smiled at me.

"No, ma'am."

"Good. Well, I can take it from here, darlin'. You can explore around outside or look around the house or go to your room or anything you'd like to do."

"Thank you," I said, turning towards the door.

"Oh, and Catherine?"

"Yes?"

"How'd you like to ride into town tomorrow and buy some fabric? You'll need some more practical dresses to wear around, I'm sure, and in town, there are some pretty prints we can buy. We can sew you some new clothes to wear. I bet you can tell we aren't fashion's angels 'round here. You see that laundry basket sitting over there? There's a simple cotton dress you can wear this evening if you want."

"Thank you, Mrs. Walter. And, I have my own money, so I can purchase my own dresses."

Mrs. Walter nodded. "Now run along."

~

After slipping into the lightness of the cotton dress, I thankfully was able to emerge outside into fresh air. I wanted to be alone. The past couple days were ultimately filled with sorrow and tears; I wanted to get away from that. I wanted to think. Glancing down at the dress I wore, I marveled at how extremely comfortable and lightweight it was, made out of pure, soft cotton. At first it felt a little funny, without the heaviness of petticoats and the tightness of a corset, and it was like I was forgetting something. The more and more time spent without those things, though, the more free I felt.

With the breeze tangling in my curls and the fresh air pumping through my veins, I decided to take a walk to explore the farm. I ran through the tall corn fields and greeted the horses in the stables. Later I walked around the garden, thinking intently. It still amazed me that I wasn't home anymore. That I was somewhere clear across the country, living a new life with a new family. So many things had happened to me so soon, and my mind was so jumbled up and knotted together. I desperately needed to untangle it all.

Taking my exploration further, I marched up the grassy hills that went for miles behind the house. They were truly the ideal place for thinking. Lush, emerald grass rolled on forever, and the luminous sky overhead sent my spirits soaring to their safety. Their earth called out my name it seemed, so I answered back by running up to the highest hill. The knoll overlooked a crystal blue spring, wide and flowing with playful waves and splashing water. It lazily connected to a huge, blue-green lake dotted here and there with green lily pads. I found it difficult to be sad in such a place.

"How beautiful!" I whispered in awe, letting my feet fly me down to the cool spring, where I unlaced my boots and lifted my skirt, gently stepping in, letting the coolness of the water ripple around my ankles and curl between my toes. Little colorful rocks bathed beneath my feet, and tiny minnows rushed away from me, inching slowly back just moments later. A silvery laugh escaped from my tummy, and I marveled at the delicious feeling of laughter. I yanked up my skirts to wade deeper. When the tips of my shins brushed the smooth water, I heard a soft humming sound coming from behind a tree on the other side of the spring. Squinting in the twilight, I could see a figure lying on the grass, back against the trunk of a tall Maplewood. I quickly ducked, trying to hush the disturbed waters as I hurried out of the spring long before I wanted to. I couldn't see who was humming, but I had a pretty good idea of who it was. I had to get away. I didn't want another confrontation. I had enough of those for one day. Just after I laced the last boot, the soft song stopped abruptly, and I sat motionless as the black figure stood out from behind the tree. Jonathon looked me up and down, hands in the pockets of his overall trousers. I rose to my full height as well, brushing the crumbles of dirt of the skirt of the dress.

I made a little, awkward motion with my hand. "I am sorry to have disturbed you. I'll leave now . . ."

He shook his head and looked around him. "I just didn't know you followed me."

I quirked an eyebrow, scoffing. "I most certainly did not follow you. I was just looking around at everything."

He nodded. "Ah. This must be a sight for you. I'm sure you didn't have trees or water or grass back home, did you?"

His sarcastic tone put me on edge. "I can see you are irritated by my presence, sir. So I'll leave you now. Sorry to have interrupted you."

"Apology accepted. So long."

I shot him a tart look before tipping my chin up and stalking away. How frazzled and irritated he had managed to make me after such a short conversation! And only a few meaningless words spoken, too! Well what did I expect from a farm boy, after all? One who had obviously been spoiled and let free to run like a wild little monster as a child. I concluded that that was why he was so unpleasant. After climbing the atrocious hill that overlooked the spring, my mind whirled and grew fuzzy. All I wanted to do was lay down. I just needed to rest a bit before continuing back to the house. Mapping out a nice little grassy area, I settled down on the ground, making sure I could not be seen by Jonathon. I yawned and blinked several times before reclining into the grassy blanket around me, stretching my arms up far above my body and letting my eyelids glide shut. In mere moments the starry sky I was looking up into disappeared, and I slid into a sweet, unexpected sleep.

~

A hand touched my shoulder, shaking me awake. Another fire? I wildly sprung into action, darting upwards into sitting position, confused and dazed all at the same time.

"Milly! We've got to . . ." I pronounced, breathing heavily, trailing off when I realized the only person hovering over me was Jonathon, and he looked a little concerned for my well-being. "Oh." A soft sound escaped from my lips, and I rubbed my eyes with the heels of my hands.

My unruly mane fell in heaps around my face, and I pushed them back with angry hands. I blinked my eyes in the dark, realizing the moon, the stars, and the chill night air now surrounded me. Jonathon stood, offered me a warm hand, and I took it gratefully. I don't remember what happened after that, and I certainly don't remember walking home, but when my eyes opened again I was in a warm bed and the clock read half passed four in the morning. Had Jonathon carried me all the way home? How *embarrassing*.

After that I could not sleep no matter what I did. Thoughts of my father and the fire and everything that had happened flooded my mind once more, and I cried to my heart's content. I wept and wept, wishing for someone to comfort me, wishing I hadn't freed Milly. Oh, if only she were here . . . I cried at the thought that this was my home now, that for all anybody cared, my life in Charleston never existed. And how I missed Papa! Not the Papa that drank and shut himself off from the world, the Papa that once loved and cared for his little daughter. I loved my papa. Why hadn't I ever tried to change him? To make him want to come out of his shell? I covered my whimpers with the bed quilts, stifling my cries. I didn't want anyone to hear me, because I was ashamed. If Papa was here, he'd tell me that life goes on. He'd say that life goes on no matter how much you cry, and that tears do no good for anybody. But Milly would say that you shouldn't leave your tears inside and let all the feelings get all knotted together. So what was I supposed to believe? Who was right? I didn't want anyone to know of my feelings. I *wanted* them to stay inside me. No one else needed to know of my own personal feelings. My slave friends always told me I should pour out my feelings to the Lord in prayer, but what could God possibly do for me? He couldn't bring back Papa and Milly. He couldn't rebuild my home from the black ashes that lay in its place. And until my tears put me to sleep, I wept until my eyes were parched and my body weak.

~

I awoke alarmed at a horrible screeching sound out my window. It sounded like a cat was being strangled to death. Bounding out of bed, I threw on my robe and hurried to look out my window. I could tell it was early morning because the darkness was slightly blemished with a stream of light. Below me a rooster beat its wings wildly, as if trying to scare off a predator. I couldn't make out what the animal was so shook up about. My heart beat wildly in my chest, and I stumbled to yank on my boots. I just had to do something. Descending down the staircase, I scurried out the door to see what all the commotion was about.

As I neared slowly upon the chicken coop, I saw why the poor rooster was making such a fuss. Stalking about the poor chickens was a lanky, red beast with a foaming mouth. It made the strangest sound I'd ever heard. A deep cry, almost. I took a frightened step away from the deranged beast.

Thinking fast, I sprinted back into the house, remembering the shotgun above the fireplace. Grabbing it with haste, I hurried back outside, struggling under the weight of the contraption in my arms. Aiming it to the sky, I pulled back the trigger and closed my eyes, heartbeat dominating my hearing. I was blown away by the boom of the gun, falling back onto the hard ground. When I glanced back up, I caught sight of the predator as it dashed back into the woods.

"Take that!" I exclaimed, raising a fist to the air.

Just when I was about to let out a relieved sigh, someone grabbed me around my waist and pulled me up to standing position. Jonathon.

"What in the world are you doing?" he demanded, putting a secure hold on the gun with one hand, the other wrapped securely yet carefully around my wrist, as if it might snap. I shrunk back and willingly let him take the gun out of my arms. His dark hair was tousled and his trousers and nightshirt were rumpled. I watched as he set the gun down on the ground. He tightened his hold on my wrist when I struggled to set myself free.

"You needn't be so angry! I was just—" There was a sharp peck on my leg, and I fell forward into Jonathon.

"Whoa!" He quickly caught me. I turned to see the brainless rooster at my heels, and I frantically pushed Jonathon forward, stumbling with him a few steps.

"Saving your blasted chickens is what I was doing!" I shouted, breaking away from him. "There was a red beast stalking them, and I scared him off."

He ran a frustrated hand through wavy, disheveled hair. "Well, next time wake me up if something like that happens. Understood?" he asked, blue eyes piercing.

I nodded, and without another word, he strode away. For a moment, I stood still. The rooster stared at me with its beady black eyes, cocking his head, gobble dribbling up and down.

"You're welcome." I murmured.

~

Later that morning after a quick breakfast, Mrs. Walter drove us into town.

"It must be so hard for you." She paused, shaking her head. "You don't even know us. And now you're livin' with us. I'd like for us to be friends. We're alike, you and I. Somethin' about you reminds me of how I used to be when I was a young woman. Anyway, you're probably wondering who we are and how we got titled as your godparents. We all used to be friends. Andrew and I used to live in Charleston, and we moved when he got the notion of farming land in Missouri. Jonathon was three then, when you were born. And just a year before we left, we were chosen to be godparents to you. Oh, and you were such a beautiful baby . . . ."

I registered the information, slowly letting everything just sink in.

"And we never once visited with you after we moved. After that we heard of your mother's death and all the memories of the good times we had together started floatin' back to us, and we got sad and homesick all over again. You must miss your mama and papa pretty much."

A feeling of guilt rushed over me. Did I miss them? I missed my house, even though it hadn't been filled with the vibrancy of life and love, like in the Walter's home. I certainly missed the way my father used to love me. And I definitely missed the love from my mother, emphasis on the missed.

I chose to remain hushed and respond only in thought to Mrs. Walter. I didn't feel like getting into one of *those* conversations. I didn't know her very well yet, anyway.

Soon we reached town at its finest hour, glistening with busy people, shoppers, and dawdlers. After entering the little fabric store located on the busy strip of tiny shops, I was entranced by the many prints and designs laid out before me. Back in Charleston, I would usually go shopping with Milly, usually for silk for a dinner dress or a new pair of satin gloves. Today I was shopping with my godmother, choosing fabrics to make my own plain dresses. The idea was horribly old-fashioned, and I liked it. My gaze immediately was attracted to a sunshine-yellow, muslin fabric. I moved closer and ran my fingers across the soft woven cotton and embroidered white flowers and designs. It simply called out my name in a bright boldness.

"Hello, ladies." An older, softly rounded woman with dark, tired eyes and weathered white skin emerged from behind the counter. "May I help you?"

"Yes, please. We're here for my godchild, Catherine," Mrs. Walter smiled.

"Well let me go find some selections that might match her skin tone. These new fabrics just came in!" The lady went through a swinging door towards the back, later bursting through again carrying several bundles of prints of every rainbow shade. In the end, I decided on some light blue silk, white cotton for blouses, and the yellow that I immediately had adored. Mrs. Walter insisted that she pay for it, and after a small argument, I gave in.

"Thank you, but it really wasn't necessary for you to purchase them for me, Mrs. Walter," I gently rebuked on the slow, easy ride home.

"Nonsense, child," Mrs. Walter said. "And please call me Anna."

~

At home, Anna and I quickly got to work, stationing ourselves in the living room and sewing to our heart's delight. Well, to Anna's delight. Sewing wasn't particularly my favorite leisure time. As I wasn't the best in the subject, Anna offered me hints and tips that I would have never considered. While I worked on a white blouse, Anna stitched up a beautiful skirt of the soft, yellow muslin. My concentration was firmly focused on sewing the blouse, while Anna seemed not even to look at what her hands were doing; it was so natural for her. We conversed and laughed together, and my heart sprang alive with happiness for a friend, something I hadn't experienced in a long while. Was Anna my new friend? Suddenly, I thought back to the day I arrived, and a haphazard question popped out of my mouth.

"On the day I came here," I looked up from my lap. "You asked the servant about a baby?"

"Nathaniel? Oh yes. His wife, Nina, just had a baby boy. They have a little daughter, too. You know they live in the servant's quarters, those cabins a little ways from the house."

I thought hard, nodding. I had never noticed the cabins, though.

"I visited them last night while you were out. Such a cute little thing. Jonah is his name, I think."

I nodded again.

"You see, those families are workers. We pay them for their hard work around the fields and the farm, and they stay on our property. They're all very kind and good-hearted. Catherine, I know you've been brought up differently than I have, as I knew your daddy. I know I have no right to try and change the way you think. But I believe they're people, too. We're all the same on the inside."

I remained silent, concentrating on the fabric in my hands.

"You play piano?" Anna asked a moment later after sensing my discomfort.

Papa had bought me lessons when I was younger, since Mother said it was expected of all young ladies to have some musical talent. At first, the thought of learning how to play the piano piqued my interest, and I was so excited to learn how. When I got it though, I was intimidated and shy, unwilling to even try. I was always worrying about upsetting Mother, making her dislike me even more, and the jumbled up black and white markings on the sheet music were confusing to me. To my surprise, however, reading music came easy to me. I looked forward to my lessons and learning songs. I adored how the smooth white keys felt beneath my fingers, the way each one played a different joyous note. I loved the way I could magically string them together to make a harmony of a song and a symphony of music.

"Yes, quite well, actually. I learned when I was a child," I answered, proudly smiling. If I could be boastful of something, it would have to be my talent of piano, and maybe drawing, too.

"Well, goodness darlin'! There's a piano right there. Play me somethin'," Anna excitedly told me, smiling from ear to ear. "That piano hasn't seen a musician in years. My daughter . . ."

Her voice trailed off, and I looked up, startled at her pale face. When she looked at me, her eyes were filled with sorrow and appeared blank, as if I was a ghost and she saw right through me. She shook her head and continued with the needlework.

"You see, I had a little girl. She died about a year ago, come this December. She was ice-skating on the lake with Jonathon, and she fell through and . . . and he tried to help her, but . . ."

My memory flashed back to yesterday when Jonathon and I were at the lake. He'd been so protective of it. He hadn't wanted me there. And now I knew why. It was the place where his beloved sister took her last breath.

"We all had been so fond of her. Jonathon simply adored her. She would be about your age if she was still living. Oh, and how she loved piano . . ." Anna looked into the distance, smiling sadly, her eyes filled with unshed tears. "I loved her . . ."

I could feel my throat go scratchy and dry. Tears rushed to my eyes, and I quickly blinked them away. Without a sound, I rose and went to the mahogany piano. Although visibly used, I was instantly drawn to its modesty. I let my fingers trail along the worn keys as I sat on the cushioned bench. Letting my hands guide me, I wistfully played my favorite, Beethoven's "Für Elise". My long tapered fingers tapped out the song, skipping over then back, over then back. I tuned the whole world out as I always did when I played piano, including my own life and everyone in it. My heart spilled out through the keys, letting every part of me go free and without hesitation. I hummed to myself, carefully pressing each key at the precise time. After I played well into the song, I looked up to see not only one pair of eyes on me, but three pairs. Before I could gasp, an applause rung through the house, and I flushed a deep pink. No one had ever praised me like this. Mother had just always expected it, and it felt good to be made over like this.

"How did you learn to play so beautifully?" asked Mr. Walter.

"I took lessons when I was a child, sir," I said, looking down at my fingers that still rested on the keys. "I love to play."

"Simply amazing, Catherine. And you don't have to be so formal. Call me Andrew."

"All right," I smiled, looking up at my godfather. I could see the kindness in his wise eyes.

Jonathon stood in the doorway, leaning against the wall with one shoulder. Something was visible on his face, was it surprise? No, not surprise. Admiration? Well, not exactly. He met my gaze, and amazingly, he smiled. Not just a smug grin, an actual *smile*. It was a wondrous thing, and dimples dotted his cheeks, bringing his whole face into a bright glow. My insides churned and I felt weak at all this commendation. Breaking the spell, I stood and smiled again at Anna, who took me in her arms and cried.

"Oh, Catherine," she whispered. "Dear Catherine . . ."

~

That night, I sat in my room and sketched out the horse that was silently chewing on grass in the pasture. It was my favorite, the one with the paint splotches. Secretly, I named her Belle. I watched in astonishing silence as the pony neighed gently, bending its long neck to chew on blades of grass. Carefully and quietly, I penciled in just the right amount of shading to her patches, catching the twinkle of her eyes and the strength of her body. When I finished, I sat admiring my work, marveling at my masterpiece. I had taken a simple moment of beauty, and captured it on paper. After gazing at the horse for several moments, I put away my sketchbook and my pencil and went to bed. Not one tear escaped from my eye that night, and I was asleep before I could think any wretched thoughts. In a moment, sleep took over again, and I drifted lazily into an ocean-deep, starry slumber.

~

After a hearty breakfast of toast and strawberry jam, eggs, and bacon, I went outside with my sketchbook. I wanted to draw a scene of the lake and the lilies in the grass knoll that surrounded it. I offered to help Anna with my dress, but she insisted it would only take a second for her to finish it up. Well good. I didn't like to sew much anyway. I inhaled the fresh air. A cool, summery breeze swept up my hair, making my spirits soar with the little birds overhead. It was such a gorgeous day, with warm sunshine and bright skies. Looking over to my right, I saw the huge fields and the laboring workers in them. Then I saw Andrew—who worked alongside Nathaniel—wave a hand generously my way, so I waved back. Jonathon worked a little farther up the fields, scooping up some rich, black earth with a shovel. He was working hard, I could tell, because sweat glistened on his bare back.

When I reached the lake, I heard the sound of a child's rambunctious laughter. It caught my attention, and so I dared to venture farther. I neared upon a tidy little village, it seemed, of log cabins. The servants' quarters, I presumed. So this is where they lived. I planned on turning around before I got too close, but just as I was about to do so, a scene caught my eye. Two Negro children ran around in the grass outside one of the nearest cabins, one chasing the other. The little boy being chased held a tiny doll of some kind, and the girl was frantically hollering at him to give it back.

"Toby! Gimme back Angela! Give 'er back!" she yelled, tears springing out of her eyes. I couldn't ignore the act of injustice.

"Excuse me!" I yelled when I was only a few steps away. "Give her back her doll, please."

Immediately the boy stopped and looked down at his bare feet. "Sorry, ma'am."

"It's all right." I felt a kind of pity for the boy at his guilty reaction. Coming closer, I saw the doll the girl held was no more than a corn cob with some cloth scraps for clothes.

"What's your name?" I asked the girl.

"Lacy," she said, shying a little away. Just then, I recognized her as the little girl that had followed one servant around. The daughter of the man who had driven us that day. She held out her hand, lifting only four of her fingers. "I'm four."

I bit back a chuckle.

"And you are?" I motioned to the boy.

He got all tough, standing up straight and puffing out his chest, saying,

"I'm Toby Mason Jasper. I live right over there." He pointed to the house right next to the one we stood in front of.

"So you two are neighbors?" I asked of Toby, who looked no older than six or seven.

"Yeah, we is."

"I got a brother!" Lacy unpredictably yelled, jumping up and down. "A baby one! Wanna see 'im?"

Anna had told me his name. Jonah, was it? I shook my head at her offer. "I don't think—"

But before I could utter a response, both children had stormed into the cabin, leaving little choice for me but to follow them.

"Hello?" I asked when I was inside. The only light in the house was a single stream of sunshine floating through the windows.

"Hullo," came a soothing voice. It reminded me of Milly's. Deep and like velvet. "Are you Missus Anna's god baby?"

"Yes." After my eyes adjusted I could see the form of a woman cradling a tiny sleeping baby in her hands. "Yes, I am. I'm Catherine."

"Well, I ain't gonna get up now with this sleeping baby, Catherine, so come here," the woman said. "Ah, there you are! You're very pretty."

I forced a smile. I felt very uncomfortable to be there. Back in Charleston, I was never allowed close to where the slaves lived. "Thank you."

"Mommy! 'Dis is my nice friend."

Friend? I bit my lip. She was a cute girl, after all.

"Well, good to meet you, nice friend," the woman said. "I'm Nina. Nathaniel's my husband. You mighta met 'im already."

"Yes, I have." I was about to excuse myself, when Nina's voice stopped me again.

"So, how old are you?"

"Seventeen." There was something about this woman, such a calm air about her that reminded me of Milly. Nina even looked like her, with the big, brown eyes and the full lips and high-cheekbones.

"Well," I offered, moving closer to the door, "I better not disturb you any longer. Goodbye."

"Mhm. Thanks for settlin' that fight between these two out there! I would've, if not for this sleepin' baby in my lap."

As I made my way back to the lake, I scolded myself. Why had I felt the need to go down there? Highly unacceptable. I suppose it wasn't quite the same as the slaves' cabins, though. I shook off the idea and soaked in the beautiful picture spread out wide before me. My eyes feasted on the rich pastures and the cool, shimmering, blue waters. The lilies and the wild flowers that dotted the hills made the gorgeous landscape complete. Not wasting a moment longer, I flipped to a fresh, white sheet of paper and began my sketch with the lake in the center. It was to be my point of emphasis. And then I shaped out the tall grass that surrounded it, the tiny spring that flowed from it. I drew the single tree that stood by the spring, the giant oak that seemed to boast, *Yes, I'm one magnificent tree!*

As I drew, I began to relax. I felt my muscles relinquish the harbored anxiety and stress with every breath I took of the sweet air. After what seemed like an eternity, my drawing was finished. I chided myself when I remembered that I'd forgotten to bring the watercolors. I don't know why, but Milly had thrown all my art tools, brushes, pencils, and paints in my luggage the day of the fire. At any rate, I'd have to finish the drawing later from memory. The wonderful day must have done something to me, because suddenly, I had a surge of energy and wanted to put it to good use. Anna had said something of wash day when I talked with her that morning at breakfast. Wash! I could do that! I'd never washed clothes before, but I'd seen the scrub maid, Lola, working at the task back home. It couldn't be that hard. I gathered up my sketchbook and strode off, inhaling big gulps of the air and enjoying the colorful freedom around me. In a minute, I found myself skipping! Not a proper thing for a lady to do, but honestly, who cared? I reluctantly stopped my jovial skip into a walk, so as not to turn heads when I passed the fields.

Sure enough, when I reached the house, Anna had a big wooden tub stationed in the backyard. She was leaning over the tub, which was filled to the brim with soapy water and suds, and I saw the routine way she selected a shirt or pair of trousers, then dunked it in the bucket and scrubbed it on the washboard. After viewing how she moved the wet clothes to hang on a clothes' line above, I decided to make my appearance known.

"Hello, Anna," I offered a slight smile. What if she refused my help? She probably thought me incapable of any real work. "Do you need my help?"

She looked up, face flustered and surprised. "Oh, hello, darlin'. By all means. I'd be grateful."

I moved past her, chose a skirt from the soiled clothes pile, and scooped up a spare washboard. Then, I followed her example and sent it under the water, using the washboard as though I'd been doing it my whole life. After that, I rang out the skirt and reached high, pinning it onto the wooden pins.

"What made you decide you wanted to help?" Anna asked, grabbing a shirt.

"Well," I said, reaching for a pair of trousers. "I must learn these things. I . . . well, I'm going to live here and I need to help with the chores. I can see there is plenty to be done."

"You're right," she chuckled.

"I'm sorry I don't know much about anything."

"Honey, don't apologize. Listen, I grew up in Charleston, you know. Yes ma'am, I was quite the city girl. And then I met Andrew Walter." She laughed out loud. "Oh, yes, I was sixteen and he was nineteen. He was visitin' some kinfolk that lived in Charleston for the summer, when he really lived here in St. Louis. So anyway, we met by mistake and fell in love and eloped. Ah, and my parents! How angry they were! But, I loved Andrew, and we were young and foolish. But we haven't been separated from the day we've married, so I know I did the right thing."

I smiled at her love story. It sounded so romantic and rebellious.

"And then after we married, my parents decided they weren't goin' to let me be a farm girl, so they gave me and Andrew enough money to buy a nice house in Charleston. And then we met your parents not much later and Jonathon came along. Well, and then you were born and your parents made me and Andrew the godparents, and then our trio moved here, because Andrew's yearnin' for home got too strong. Well, and then my daughter, Anna Mae, came along, and we all just sort of felt at home in St. Louis."

"Forbidden love," I whispered.

Anna let out a silvery laugh. "You could say that. Well, looks like we're done with this job! Oh, I finished your dress! Come see!"

I followed Anna through the house and into my bedroom, where my dress laid on the bed quilt. It looked so wonderfully light and comfortable that I longed to wear it. Nearing closer, my fingertips traced the little designs and flowers sewed into the cotton blouse and the yellow skirt.

"Thank you," I mused, hovering over the dress. It certainly wasn't anything I was used to wearing, but it looked like heaven.

"If you can wait to wear it until Sunday when we go to church, that will be fine. You can keep on wearing my dresses until then," Anna said before turning to leave. "I'm going to fix some lunch for Andrew and Jonathon, and we all can have ourselves a picnic."

I looked wistfully to my new dress before eagerly slipping it on. Marveling at myself in the mirror, I found that the beautiful skirt and blouse fit perfectly. Anna certainly did have a way with needle and thread.

~

"Comin'?" Anna asked when I entered the kitchen. Her hair was caught up in a bonnet, and she swayed a straw basket in her hand.

Both of us strolled outside, instantly met with the gentle, cool breeze of summer. Anna called out to Jonathon and Andrew, telling them to meet us down by the lake. Andrew, far out in the fields, waved in reply. I watched in curiosity as Negro men and women trailed back towards the servants' cabins. I supposed it was their lunchtime, too.

"The servants and Andrew and Jonathon work every day, almost. Except Sunday, you know. They are especially busy this month, since harvestin' is only in about a week. This season brings so many festivities!"

"What kind of festivities?" I asked. I was beginning to feel very comfortable around Anna. She was the kind of person that you had to like.

"Well, we'll have the husking bee. It'll be so nice for you. You'll get to meet all sorts of people and make friends, because believe it or not, this town is crawling with young people like yourself. Honestly. Oh, I know you'll make friends. There are plenty of young ladies to meet. And young men, I daresay."

Smiling, I climbed the green hill that elegantly hung over the blue lake. Jonathon and Andrew beat us there and collapsed playfully into the soft grass at the top, bodies shaded by a tall, magnificent tree.

"What did you bring?" Andrew asked.

"Just be patient, Andrew," Anna replied. "You'll find out soon enough."

Jonathon laughed, and my heart did something strange at the sound of it. Suddenly aware of myself, I gathered my skirts and sat down next to Andrew. We all watched with watering mouths as Anna pulled out sandwiches, apples, and a boatload of cookies for dessert. A smile tugged at my lips when Jonathon's persisting hand reached hastily for a cookie. Anna slapped his hand away.

"Jonathon, always use manners when you're in the presence of a lady," Anna chided. "Right, Catherine?"

I decided to play along. After a dainty bite of the tip of my carrot, I agreed. "Yes, of course, and there are *two* ladies here today."

Jonathon stared at me with curious eyes, watching me as I chose the largest cookie, the one he had grabbed for. I smiled as I dug my teeth into its sugary goodness, aware of the smiling eyes on me. Except Jonathon's weren't smiling.

His face seemed to say, *I haven't figured what you're all about yet, but when I do, I'll get you back. Just wait.* And I had no reason to believe he wouldn't follow through with that notion.

~

Soon Sunday arrived, and my nerves quickly set in, as I was to meet nearly the entire town for the first time. Getting ready first thing, I hurried downstairs, summoned by a delicious aroma of one of Anna's' breakfasts. As I rounded the corner after the last stair, though, I came into full contact with Jonathon, and I was propelled backwards. Immediately, I felt a hot rush spill down my blouse. Steadying myself, I glanced down, disturbed at what I saw. An ugly black stain of coffee drenched me, and my skin was burning hot. I let out a horrified cry.

"Are you all right?" Jonathon inquired, taking hold of me to get me back on my feet. Anna rushed over to me, shaking her head.

"What a shame! Well, 'tis no matter. I can clean it out. Just throw it into the wash basket."

"It's true! She can get any out any stain from here to New York. Honestly," Jonathon assured me, a red flush crawling its way up his neck.

I nodded and turned, rushing up the stairs. How terribly horrifying! And now what would I wear? The only other choice was to dress in one of my gowns I'd purchased in Charleston. I pouted, stripping off the blemished blouse and skirt. Opening the cherry-mahogany wardrobe, I filed through several dresses. After a minute, I reluctantly decided on the lavender dress. It was the plainest of them all. But by no means was it plain. Oh no! It had its share of ruffles and frilly lace.

As I slipped it over my head, I shivered as the cool tissue taffeta brushed my skin. I fingered the bodice, decorated with embroidered gold designs dotted with beadwork. I decided it was much too extravagant for the Walters' taste, but it was the best option. What a disappointment, though. All the hard work on that dress and coffee is spilled all over it. Poor Anna.

"Goodness!" Anna whispered when I entered the kitchen. Her eyes bulged, and she came running over to feel the ruffle skirts and tiny beadwork. "Glory be!"

"I know it's a little much, but I—"

"No, no. It'll be fine. Just fine," Anna assured me, beaming over the dress the way chickens go crazy once chicken feed is down. Under her breath, she murmured, "I remember when I used to wear things like this."

"I don't miss it," I countered, smiling. I then took my place at breakfast. Andrew read his paper, glancing up once to say good morning. I saw Jonathon staring at me from the corner of my eye, and I suddenly felt out of place. If I felt like that at the Walters' table, I would most certainly feel that way at church. After we said grace, everyone started digging in to a gravy and buttermilk biscuits breakfast. The biscuits were so light and flaky, and the gravy was so creamy and tasty, that I forgot all about my dress, and decided that it all was going to be fine.

Once Jonathon hitched up the buggy team, we all climbed up into the seats, and I honestly thought I had ants crawling on my backside. If I was this bad now, I would probably be jumping up and down come time for church service. Oh! And I hadn't attended *church* in a long while. Honestly, I think the last church service I sat through was Mother's funeral . . .

Andrew took the reins in his own palms, to my surprise. As if she read my mind, Anna explained the reason.

"If you're wonderin' why Nathaniel isn't driving us today, I'll tell you that he doesn't usually drive us at all. He offered to take us into town that day you met us. He has his own church service to go to today."

We winded around all the curves and bends in the little road that peeked over everything the Walters owned. Peering out the window, I looked towards the servants' cabins in the distance. People were beginning to congregate in the middle of the two rows of houses, sitting on various wooden chairs set up in neat little aisles in front of a makeshift pulpit.

I watched as farmland gradually turned into houses and a busy little main street. A small, red-brick church stood at the end of the main street, bustling people hurrying in through its welcoming doors. Soon the carriage halted, and Andrew in his Sunday's best hopped down from the seat. He came around and opened the door for us ladies like a gentleman should. Somehow, I could imagine him as someone my father would like. Actually, anyone could like him. It was no wonder he was married to Anna. They were a very agreeable match.

Jonathon hurried out behind me, and I couldn't help but notice how nice he looked in his starched shirt, tan trousers, and suspenders. His hair was nicely slicked back, and his eyes were somber and shining bright blue. And suddenly I wondered if he was sweet on anyone. Maybe he had a girl in church that he liked. No one in the family ever talked about that, but I couldn't help but be a little curious.

Clusters of smiling, nudging ladies and men made my stomach suddenly lurch and flutter, and I wished dearly to get right back in the carriage. And I would have, too, if

Anna hadn't grabbed my hand, pulling me into a circle of women, young and old alike.

"Good morning, ladies," Anna sang. "This here's my godchild, Catherine Carey."

"Hello, Catherine," a short woman grasped my hand. "I'm Mrs. Linda Akins."

"Hello," I smiled before turning to someone else that had me by the other hand.

"Well, hi! I am Josephine. Welcome to St. Louis!" Before I could respond, a million introductions were thrown my way, including curious questions and praises and whatnot. I forced a sad smile and felt suddenly faint.

"Stop," I whispered. Then louder, "Please..." And when they didn't stop, I became so overwhelmingly frustrated I couldn't take it. But they did not stop. I looked all around for Anna, who more than likely had been swallowed up by these crazy ladies she called friends. But then, the loud resounding of church bells rung through the air, and all the women said their goodbyes to me, joining their families and marching toward the church's doors. I let out a puff of relief and looked all about me to find a familiar face. Just then, a strong hand took me steadily by the elbow, and I looked up to see Andrew.

"Oh, thank goodness it's you, Andrew! All those ladies left me no peace."

He chuckled, leading me into the church with Anna and Jonathon close behind.

"I know. Don't tell Anna I said so, but I feel sorry for some of them gals' husbands."

Andrew led me carefully to a pew in the very middle. The church wasn't anything like I remembered my old one to be. It was smaller, and it had about ten rows of individual cushioned pews, and the church itself appeared to be very old. But it was a friendly place, nonetheless. Looking around, I saw children and elderly couples, middle-aged people and infants. But what I saw most of was young people around my age. Most of them stared at me, gaping at my attire as if they saw right through me. Hadn't they ever seen a purple dress before? Goodness, you'd think I was a toad the way their eyes bore into me like that. I quickly looked away, eyes focusing on the elderly preacher dressed in white robes standing before the congregation. When he began to speak, I couldn't help but be drawn to him, to his words, like a fish on a hook. His persona demanded that sort of attention from people.

"Friends and Neighbors," he began in a voice that held me accountable almost automatically. "Welcome to the house of the Lord. Today the sun shines bright, showing God's love for His children below. Please rise and let us call ourselves to worship."

"That's Pastor Dominic," Anna whispered to me as we stood.

"Dear God, we thank You for this day and all of the blessings you have so graciously given us. Help us to love our neighbors and treat one another fairly, and let us love each other as we love ourselves. Help us to live our lives the right way, Your way, and let each one of us find our purpose on earth. Continue to bless us and love us, dear Lord, and keep each one of us in your capable hands. In Jesus's name we pray, Amen. Please be seated."

I did so, listening carefully for the preacher's next words.

"The Lord God made us all equal. He didn't make one man weaker or stronger than the next . . . ."

Carefully, I absorbed his every word. Although I did not understand everything he said, my curiosity had been piqued. His speech had revolved around equality for all men. Except Negroes, I projected. At the end of the service, I stood by Anna while she mindlessly chatted to her friends and introduced me to each one. There were more glances shot my way, and I saw a group of girls my age whisper and send questioning looks my way. Jonathon was standing in a group of young men not far away, and even they sent inquiring and scrutinizing glances toward me. I quickly averted my gaze, but out of the corner of my eye I saw Jonathon's eyes on me, just watching me. And then the woman Anna was talking to referred to a boy in Jonathon's group, and he came striding over, bringing himself up to his full height, puffing his chest out with the utmost confidence.

"Yes, Mother?" he inquired.

"I'd like you to meet Anna's godchild, Catherine," the woman said, smiling my way.

He nodded at me, and I forced a smug smile. "Nice to meet you, Catherine. I'm William Andrews."

I nodded back, sizing him up. He wasn't as tall as Jonathon, as he was stocky with a steady gaze and a head full of blonde hair. He had green eyes, an interesting shade of green with a spark of gold hidden in them. He was handsome, but not like Jonathon was. Glancing over my shoulder, I saw Jonathon watching us with a face of . . . what? I couldn't tell. But I thought I saw the slightest bit of — dare I say it — jealousy? Of course not. Whyever jealousy? Anyway, I didn't care. I was more concerned with getting back to the house. So when Andrew announced our leave, I was quick to be the first one out.

On the ride home, Anna chattered heedlessly, telling me how everyone loved me already and how she thought secretly that all the young men were sweet on me. I didn't give my full attention to it all, trying to sum up what *I* thought about the day at church. The service had been interesting enough. The preacher's words haunted me though. He had been talking about equality. Equality among white men, right? I hoped so. If the Walters' attended a church full of abolitionists, I don't think my conscience would permit me to attend. I told myself I wouldn't let it bother me. Ignorance is bliss. Besides, he wasn't really talking about slavery, just fairness. So I needn't worry. And it was like that all the way home, Jonathon staring blankly out the window, Andrew with an amused smile on his satisfied face, and Anna with her foolish, endless talking.

~

That night, I again drew the horse I named Belle. My thoughts were far away, though, not fully focused on my sketch. My mind traveled back to church, back to all the strange looks Jonathon had given me. Had he been jealous of the attention I'd received? I felt as though he secretly hated me, and I didn't know why.

Then I thought about the servant families down in the log cabins. They reminded me so much of my slaves back home, and I felt a sort of tenderness towards them. I thought of Nina, the kind and gentle woman that reminded me so much of Milly. And her baby! He was so fragile and darling. My heart especially went out to little Lacy, who had the most thoughtful eyes I'd ever seen. And then I thought of her rag doll. What a shame, it was scarcely a doll at all. Maybe I would sew her a real one . . . Anyway, there was no harm in trying to make friends with the servants. Negroes or not, they were my only options for friends at the present.

~

The next morning I awoke to women's laughter. It certainly wasn't Anna making all that noise, for I heard many different high-pitched voices conversing rather loudly. What in the world was going on? Peeping downstairs in just my robe, I saw a whole group of ladies, ranging from sixteen years of age to eighty. They all sat around the living room, chatting and sewing up a storm. A quilting circle perhaps? Why hadn't Anna warned me? I hurried back up the stairs, quickly cleaning myself up. Hurrying to dress, I thought of my pretty new ensemble that was now hanging outside on the clothesline all by its lonesome. Anna had managed to get the stain out, after all.

I slipped on my silky jade gown, lacing up my boots before fixing my tresses. Then, I pinched my cheeks, something Milly had taught me how to do long ago when Papa said I was far too young for rouge.

Composing myself, I daintily lifted my skirts and descended down the stairs. My gown made a soft rustling sound as I entered the room, and I became aware of all the inquisitive pairs of eyes on me.

"Catherine! I thought you'd never wake!" laughed Anna, coming to me.

I wanted to yell, *Why didn't you tell me of this beforehand?* But I thought better of it, and instead, I smiled gently, saying, "May I join you?"

"Oh, of course. See, this is the Ladies Sewing Circle." She turned to me, and softly, in my ear, she said "We meet twice every month, and I would have told you, but I forgot myself. See, this morning when I was drinkin' my coffee, here comes a whole parade of ladies up my driveway, so I rush up to change and I look in on you. And you're just sleepin' so nice that I don't bother to wake you. Now don't go tellin' those women I forgot, because they'll be saying things about me bein' forgetful. And that's the last thing I want to be named. Now come sit down."

"This is Catherine, ladies," Anna said to a group of younger ladies.

"Hello," one said, encouraging the rest to follow.

"I'm sure they'll let you sit with them, right girls?" asked Anna, smiling broadly.

"Of course!" another exclaimed, urging me to sit. And so I tucked my skirts and took a place on a small area of carpet. Anna handed me sewing materials. Sighing, I looked around at the circle. There were five girls, including myself, and they all gaped at me, as if just waiting to see if I'd blink.

"How do you do," I whispered, forcing a tiny smile.

"Why, just fine!" chirped the one to my right. She was slightly plump, with wide, turquoise eyes and raven-black hair. I felt as though she was kind from the start, with her twinkling eyes and generous smile. "I'm Mallory. I saw you at church yesterday, though you probably didn't see me. Oh, how beautiful you look in all your dresses! My, I only wear gowns like that on very special occasions." She gasped then, hands fluttering to her mouth. Then in a soft voice, she placed a hand over mine and said, "I'm so sorry about your loss. My mother told me."

"Oh, it's all right. Thank you." I was wondering if Anna had told them yet why I had come. I got my answer. It didn't bother me at all; I'd rather Anna tell everyone than me have to.

Later on, I knew every girl's name there. There was Mallory, of course, and a silly red-head named Laura, a quiet girl called May, and, from what I could tell, a stuck-up brunette who I think was used to being center of attention. Her name was Rosalie Andrews, sister to William, the boy I'd met at church, and daughter to a rich factory owner. Her eyes were like two blueberries, and her lips were tight and prim and painted bright red. Honestly, I didn't like her after one minute of being next to her. Whenever she spoke, she made an effort to bounce her corkscrew curls and flash one of her dimpled smiles. Of course, I wouldn't let a silly girl like this get to me. I knew my place.

"So, you're from Charleston?" she asked, neatly crocheting something with pink and blue stripes.

"Yes."

"I hear it's very crowded there. Am I right?"

"Well, I—"

"And so now you live with Mrs. Walter?"

"I do."

"Well, I live a little ways from here in that big three-story you've probably seen. I'm sure you've seen it. My daddy runs a huge factory in the city, you know. I am very fond of your dress. Do you like mine?" Rosalie looked down to her attire, which was a muslin dress, the color of lemonade. Inwardly, I groaned. Luckily though, Mallory saved me just in time.

"I'm sure you'll like it here, Catherine. There's lots of fun things to do. Well you know next week the corn husking is going on. And of course there are always dances and such to attend. And church is always nice, when we get to see everybody—"

"My family is going to be hosting several more parties this year," Rosalie boasted, nose sticking straight up. "Including the Annual Autumn Fling. Everybody always says our parties are the best. It's true. Right May?"

The shy blonde flinched and then nodded a little.

Soon, the sewing party ended, and I joined the Walters out in the fields after a quick change of clothes. Today was tomato picking day, Anna told me, so she and I took a long, calming walk down to the garden. It was a peaceful morning, with happy birds chirping and the crispness of autumn just beginning to take form. It was a tad cooler, with soft breezes and white, puffy clouds. Anna and I gossiped about everyone there, and she told me who was a potential friend and who to avoid.

"Watch out for Mrs. Brissel. She isn't the nicest lady around, and that's all I'll tell you about that," Anna warned me in a hushed tone.

"What about that Rosalie?" I asked, looking up into the swirling puffs of white clouds.

"Rosalie? Humph!" I could tell Anna was getting a little out of breath. "Rosalie Andrews is the only daughter of the wealthiest family in St. Louis. They don't live very far from here, you know. Oh, I was chatting with Mrs. Andrews on Sunday, and you met the son, didn't you? Rosalie's parents are quite kind people; it's only Rosalie who's the spoiled egg of the family, if you know what I mean."

"And Mallory?"

"Oh, a sweet girl. Her mother and I are good friends."

"Yes, I like her, also. She seemed very kind."

At last we came upon the rows of ripe tomatoes, and each of us made our way down the vines, picking the ripe ones and placing them in baskets. My, how many there were!

"Anna?" I called.

"Yes?"

"What kind of chores shall I do around here?" I asked. I felt as though I needed a better place in the house. I needed to do more. Perhaps a list of duties to carry out daily would keep me busy and make me feel like I was put to good use.

"Well, you already are a great help with all the household things."

I shook my head. "I feel like I need to do more . . ."

"I'm sure Jonathon could use your help with the animals."

"That sounds fine. I'll start tomorrow."

~

I should have never agreed to it.

Before the sun had even had a chance to peek its way over the horizon, someone knocked heavily on my door. I must have been only subconsciously aware, for what seemed like an eternity later there were more furious knocks. Oh, but the bed felt so good, and I was so warm and deliciously comfortable that I just rolled over and drifted away again. Besides, it was still dark. And I was still tired.

A second later, my door flung open and someone stormed into the room. I reluctantly opened my eyes to see Jonathon peering down at me.

"We have to milk the cows now," he said moderately. "Mama told me you wanted to help."

A pang of fury washed over me. What was he thinking, coming in my bedroom like this?

"What are you doing in my room?" I asked through gritted teeth. "Get out."

His eyebrows knitted together, and his jaw tightened. I pulled the quilt close around me.

"Do you know how improper this is?" I inquired.

"You wanted to help, and I would have never come in if you had woken up like you were supposed to. I'll give you a few minutes to get dressed and then we'll go. All right?"

I was so tired I could barely nod in reply. My head weighed a ton and I could feel my eyelids slowly press down. Farther, and farther. And farther. I vaguely saw him leave, heard the sound of a door shutting. After that, I lazily drifted back away into a cozy slumber. Who cares about the cows? Who cares about . . . I was asleep again, but not for long.

A rush of cold water splashed over my face. I cried out and shot out of the bed, hair limp and face dripping. Jonathon stood in front of me, water pail in hand. He grinned mischievously and whistled, strolling his way out of my room.

"Get dressed," he ordered before shutting the door closed. He was mad. Absolutely mad.

With angry, sharp movements, I yanked on one of Anna's old dresses and shoved my feet into my walking boots. After fully dressed, I strode out of my room and scurried down the stairs. Jonathon waited at the bottom, a knowing grin on his face.

"Sleep well, Miss Carey?" he asked with false sincerity.

"Oh yes," I said sarcastically, brushing past him. "Nothing like a cold splash of water to start the day. And yourself?"

"You don't really care, do you?"

He opened the door for me, and, with my chin tilted confidently skyward, I emerged into the chilly morning air. Immediately I knew that I should have brought a shawl. The moon hung low in the sky, now just a faded white sphere muddled between dark clouds. The sky was most vulnerable, painted with gentle blue and purple streaks. The lush grass was wet with dew, and the morning seemed so soft and delicious. It was the most peaceful time of day. Dawn.

Without a word, I followed Jonathon into the barn where he let the cows go free. Like the shepherds in the bible that Milly used to talk about, we led the cows into the pastures for them to graze. Jonathon, pail and wooden stool in hand, visited an older cow that he said was one of the most temperate. He placed the stool in front of the cow's hide and sat down. With fast but gentle motions, the milk drizzled into the pail with ease. I could do this. It appeared to be simple enough.

"Think you can try?" he asked, but I saw the doubt in his blue eyes. That made me all the more determined to show him.

"Yes. I can do it."

"You sure?"

I nodded solemnly, and he rose to his feet, urging me to sit down. After doing so, I stared at the creature. It certainly wasn't like the sweet, black-spotted cows in the books Milly used to read to me. Really, they weren't sweet at all. They were intimidating. I grimaced at the way flies buzzed and landed all over her bristly body, the way she swished her violent tail back and forth, back and forth. The only thing "kind" about the creature was her eyes perhaps. They were dark and relaxed. Taking a deep breath, I prepared myself for what I'd have to do.

On the first pull, the crazed creature called Betsy mooed loudly and rammed her body against my head. I ducked and winced before Jonathon pulled me back. He was laughing.

"Well, I think she likes you, Catherine. You're a natural!"

I snorted. "It isn't funny."

He shook his head, finishing the job himself.

Hands on my hips, I watched him. What a great skill he had! Girls back home would die for a man that milked cows so wonderfully. I smiled at my own sarcasm. He went down the line, milking all seven cows and pretending I wasn't even there.

"Now for the chickens," Jonathon announced. "And about the milking, you pulled too hard. Oh, and Betsy is the most ill-tempered cow we have."

I shot him a look full of contempt.

"Betsy doesn't know quite how to be a proper lady. I think maybe you should teach her watercolors and French, or whatever it is you know how to do. Then she'll behave."

I remained hushed, as wittiness was not my specialty, especially so early in the morning. I found it more effective to stay silent, anyway.

Jonathon plopped a bag of seed into my arms once we reached the chicken coop. I buckled under its weight, and Jonathon smiled. Sloppily, I spread out the feed onto the ground, aware of Jonathon's blue gaze on me. Then he opened the coop and a couple dozen chickens came flocking out, hurrying to stuff their beaks with the feed. The rooster, who was gawking around over by the outhouse, gobbled over and tried to squeeze in for a couple morsels of food. I almost laughed out loud at the silly sight of it all.

"Now let's collect the eggs," Jonathon said, hunching into the coop. There were about thirteen of the off-white eggs, and I prided myself on the small job done correctly.

"What do we do with the eggs and milk?" I asked as he returned the bag of feed.

"Well," he said, leaning on a tree stump, "we sell some, and the milk we keep after we run it through the separator. We make butter with the cream. In the morning and in the evening, we have to milk them. We could switch alternate days back and forth once you get the hang of it. You know, I do it tomorrow and you the next day."

"All right," I agreed, smiling. "So I get to sleep in tomorrow."

A slow smile crept onto his face. For a moment, he just stared at me as if he was trying to read me like a book. If anyone needed figuring out, it was him.

"What?" I asked, folding and unfolding my arms subconsciously.

He gulped and shook his head. "Nothing. You did all right today."

~

While Anna went into town to pick up a few groceries, I stayed home and cleaned. I'd overheard her telling Andrew that the whole house needed dusting, and the floors needed mopping. Easy enough. I'd watched Lola do everything a thousand times. But before I could begin the job, I decided I needed to relieve myself. I tried to avoid going to the outhouse as much as possible, as back in Charleston, I had my own personal chamber pot. Outhouses repulsed me. But how could a body possibly avoid one for very long when it was all one had?

Hurrying outside, I scampered to the outhouse, slamming the wooden door behind me. After relieving myself, I attempted to lift the latch, but it would not budge. I pulled again with all my might, but in vain. I then tried everything, from kicking it to wiggling it. I'd used the thing many times since I'd first been here, why was it acting up now? Miss Mortemeyer had once advised to faint in a horrid, desperate situation such as this, but if I did, I'd fall face first into the latrine, and what good would that do? So I did the only other thing I could do. I screamed for help. And within a minute, the rushing sound of footsteps came thumping.

"Catherine!" someone yelled.

"Where are you?" another voice asked.

"In the outhouse! I don't know what happened, but I'm stuck!"

I heard a muffled sound of men's laughter. Squinting my eyes, I puffed out in frustration.

"It's not funny. I can't get out of here!" I exclaimed, banging the door.

"Well, well, well," I heard Jonathon say satanically, "What shall we do, men?"

I waited, listening in fury. My temper escalated with each word spoken.

"We could always try pushing the thing down. But I'm afraid she'd tumble over and get herself, well, rather dirty," another voice answered. I recognized the smooth timbre as belonging to William Andrews.

Some more muffled chuckles and the shuffle of feet ensued.

"It's worth a shot." Jonathon stated, laughing through his teeth. "All right, Will. On the count of three. One . . ."

The outhouse rocked me back and forth, and I let out a piercing scream, bracing myself.

"Jonathon! Don't!" I bellowed.

"Two . . ."

I tried screaming again, this time even louder and more shrilled.

"Wait a second!" Jonathon exclaimed, setting the outhouse back in place.

I breathed a sigh of relief.

"Catherine," he shouted, "can you hear me?"

"Yes, I can hear you perfectly well." *You swine.*

"Well, the only other option I can think of is for you to pull the latch out first towards you, and then lift it up. It's a tricky little thing."

I stared at the latch, did as I was told, and stepped out to find two pairs of malevolent male eyes upon me. Immediately, I felt my face flush red.

Jonathon and William both burst into laughter upon seeing me, and Andrew came running with a pitchfork in his hand. "What's the matter? Catherine, what's wrong?"

"She locked herself in the privy!" Jonathon hooted, conjuring up another chain of reckless howls.

And do you know what? Andrew just started laughing, too, and I became so frustrated my fists shot to my waist.

"It's not funny! You . . . you . . . you bunch of pigs! No proper gentleman would dare laugh at a lady!" And I stormed off, rushing past Jonathon and his yowling friend.

Inside, I whimpered silently to myself while finishing the cleaning.

A little before Anna came home, I went out in the barn to milk the cows, and Jonathon joined me. I ignored his advances of conversation, focusing strictly on the tedious job before me, which I was beginning to get the knack of. Amazingly, the cows were behaving for me, and Jonathon finally got the hint that I didn't like him all that much and wished he'd be quiet. Afterwards, I stole away to my bedroom and stayed there for the remainder of the evening, coming down only for dinner, ignoring Jonathon when he tried to apologize.

~

The next morning I got up early and dressed quietly so I wouldn't wake anyone up. I wanted to surprise Anna with breakfast, as I knew she deserved a break from preparing the meals she toiled over day after day. I located a few of Anna's recipes in the kitchen, deciding I would bake some fancy biscuits, since they seemed simple enough. After collecting enough eggs from the chicken coop and locating the flour and sugar in the pantry, I searched for the preserves. I raided the pantry from top to bottom, but they were nowhere in sight. Maybe the cellar? Yes, the cellar would be where they were stored. Cook used to store all sorts of canned goods in there, including a variety of fruit jellies and preserves.

I hurried outside, and a stampede of freezing air whirled about me. Pulling my shawl closer, I searched around the house for the cellar doors. Once I found them somewhere towards the back of the house, I yanked on the rusted handles that didn't want to budge. I pulled harder, and when they flung open, I landed flat on my back end.

Grunting, I righted myself back on my feet. Standing up, I brushed the crumbles of dust off my old skirts and stepped inside. It was pitch black, with only a ray of early sunlight streaming through. I kept going, trying my hardest to ignore the moldy scent. Groping my way along, I stumbled upon a wall filled with all sorts of canned goods. There were shelves and shelves of canned items like preserves, vegetables, and spices. I searched the nearest one for a couple jars of strawberry preserves, and just when my eyes caught a sight of one, a distinct human's cough sounded not so far from me. I froze, not daring to even take another breath. My heart was in my throat, and my pulse was of rapid rate. Who was with me? Who could be in the Walters' dark cellar? My heart gave a giant leap of fright, and in a moment, my whole world collapsed. My ankles snapped and I fell to the ground in a dead faint. Miss Mortemeyer would be proud that I used her method in such a desperate case as this.

~

I was shaken conscious by a pair of thick hands on my shoulders. Light flooded through the cellar as several lanterns lit up the underground room. Now I could make out every detail of the cellar. Cots and other cushioned furniture lined the walls, inhabited by dark human figures.

"You all right?" asked a woman's voice.

Immediately I jumped to my feet, heart racing all over again. After adjusting my eyes, I saw a black woman stand before me, eyes like a frightened deer's.

"We leavin'?" a man's voice asked as dark figures unfolded and emerged forward. "Not in the middle of the day."

I couldn't take it any longer. Crying out, I rushed up the cellar stairs, sprinting faster than I ever thought I could. Bursting the front door open, I ran up to Andrew and Anna's bedroom door.

"Anna! Andrew! There's . . ." I panted, my heartbeat galloping. "There are Negroes in your cellar!"

The door quickly opened, and they both stood there in their nightclothes, looking utterly disheveled and disturbed.

"In your cellar!" I cried again, breathlessly.

Anna gasped, and Andrew's jaw clenched. Neither moved, neither said a word.

"We know," Anna whispered after a minute.

"What?" I asked as if I didn't hear. But I heard perfectly.

"We know there are people in our cellar," she said, looking at me with frosty eyes.

"You . . . know?"

Andrew nodded. "They . . . they're slaves."

"What?" I said, not fully understanding. "Why? What do you . . ."

Anna took a deep breath, and I heard Jonathon's footsteps behind me. Turning, I saw him and the uncertainty in his eyes.

"She knows?" he said, his voice low and dangerous.

"They are slaves, and we're helping them escape to freedom."

I didn't know what to say. I'd heard girls back in Charleston gossiping about the "underground railroad", and I would see little blurbs about it in the newspapers. From what I knew, it was an escape route for slaves. Suddenly, the mournful song of the slaves echoed hauntingly in my mind.

"For the old man's a waitin' to carry you to freedom . . . ."

Of course! It was about freedom! It always had been about freedom! Milly hadn't wanted to be a slave and neither had Cook or Gordon or anybody. All they really wanted was to be free, and maybe they would have run away if Papa hadn't kept such a close eye on them all. And what about the law? Why, if the police knew about this, they'd surely arrest Anna and Andrew! They'd be imprisoned and maybe even hanged.

"It can't be," I hoarsely whispered. The Walters had lied to me. They'd never told me about this, and they never would have, either. I should have been used to lies by now. First Papa had lied when he said he loved me, then Milly when she said she cared about me, and now the Walters. No one really cared. No one cared at all. And just when I was about to consider God and all that church nonsense. God didn't even care. I mean, if He did, would he really have done this to me? Would he really put me under the care of liars? Of felons, who helped Negroes, of all things? No. There wasn't a God, and if there was, He was mighty cruel indeed.

Without another word, I fled the house and the farm. I ran until I could run no more. Except this time, my legs carried me away from the cornfields, away from everything belonging to the Walters. I ran along the dirt road, not looking back once. Where was I to go? Perhaps back to Charleston. Or maybe I'd just get on the next train and start a new life all by myself. Or maybe not. Maybe I just would go nowhere and let my feet go on like this forever, running, not really searching for anything, just running. When I became overwhelmingly out of breath, I stopped and hunched over, frantically grasping for breath. Life . . . goes . . . on. Life . . . goes . . . on . . . My father's words drummed out the beats of my heart.

"Where are you going?" Jonathon's concerned voice rang out from behind me. I whirled around, surprised he had followed me so far.

I didn't take his offered hand. "Why do you care?"

"Listen. You can't just always run away from everything all the time—"

"You can't tell me what I can and cannot do!" I demanded, stepping back.

"You don't understand." He moved closer, carefully, however, as if I was a wild animal that might strike.

"Understand what? That you are secretly hiding slaves illegally in your cellar? Oh yes, I understand perfectly."

"It's better than owning slaves *legally*!" He raised his voice, and I flinched. I saw the rage in his eyes, the tightness of his jaw. The passion inside of him was evident. "Slavery is wrong, and you know it!"

No, I didn't know it. "So is breaking the law!" I exclaimed.

"What about God's law?" he asked coolly. "Does God think slavery is right?"

I was fueled with more anger at his remark. "I don't know what God thinks, and I don't care."

I pivoted on my foot and began to stalk away, but his next question stopped me for some reason.

"Where will you stay?"

Deliberately, I turned to look at him. Seeing the worry on his face, the genuine concern in his blue eyes, I froze.

"I just . . . I don't understand why none of you told me about this before."

He paused, moving his gaze to observe the landscape of fields and meadow.

"I guess we thought you'd do just this."

At that moment, Andrew and Anna tore down the street on one of their horses, saddling up to my side. Andrew held the reins steadily as Anna slid down off of the horse to embrace me fully.

"I'm so sorry," she murmured into my hair.

"We knew this would happen." I heard Andrew's voice crack. Only then did I realize all three of us were crying, not including Jonathon, who I discovered, never cried.

"Sorry . . . sorry, sorry." Anna continued on, mumbling things about her being so sorry and how she wished I wouldn't be upset with her. "Come sit down. Let's us have a little discussion of this matter. All right?"

"All right." I forced a smile and a nod.

Once inside, all four of us took our places in the living room, and Anna sat closest to me, hand over mine.

"Now listen." She paused, looking intently at me. "What you just found out . . . about us havin' slaves in our cellar, well . . . we know it's a surprise to you. But you must promise me you won't tell. This is a huge secret and the sad truth of it all is we could get ourselves arrested. So you must promise." She waited for my answer that wouldn't come. I couldn't promise that. Or . . . could I? I could just pretend that it I didn't know. That I never heard of any of this. That way I wouldn't be accused if anything *did* happen. All right. I'd promise if Anna wanted me too. But only because I liked the Walters, not because I thought it was right.

"I won't tell," I said.

"Thank you, darlin'," Anna praised, squeezing my hand tight. "You see, we don't believe in slavery, as I said before. But our feelins' are so strong that we would even go against the law. Now we don't want you to get all afraid. The law rarely comes around here, and when they do, we hear from certain sources when they'll be in the neighborhood. So that way we can take every precaution."

"Right," said Andrew. "We're not the only people around here that help with the Underground Railroad. A bunch of us are in this together. And tonight . . ."

"Tonight," Andrew picked up where Anna had hesitated, "is when the slaves leave. You see, they stumbled to our doorstep only yesterday, the first slaves we'd had in weeks. And usually we fill them with a hot meal and send them on their way. But last night they asked to stay. It had been a harsh journey, and it was time for them to rest. So tonight we plan on leading them away to the Mississippi River. Another conductor will be waiting on the other side to lead them to their next stop."

I hesitated. This sounded so strange, but it was so real. There were living, breathing people in the Walters' cellar. They were illegal. Wasn't this terribly wrong? I wanted to tell myself this, make myself believe how wrong and illegal this was, but there was a lingering question in my mind that wouldn't go away. It was what Jonathon had said.

"Does God think slavery is right?"

It bothered me the way the question plagued my mind, like the way a fly keeps buzzing around your head and never flies away no matter how hard you swat at it. God didn't exist for me. At least, not anymore. And I needn't concern myself with any of this anyway. If the Walters wanted to break the law, then let them. It wasn't for me to say.

~

That night, Anna sent me to bed early, telling me that I wouldn't have to worry at all about what Andrew and Jonathon planned on doing. So I obeyed reluctantly, deciding to force sleep upon myself if it didn't come instantly. But the plan didn't work so well at all, and so in the end I laid silently in bed, listening carefully to all the sounds of the night. I was hoping for the scampering of feet across the grass, the voices of Jonathon and Andrew as they called out to the slaves. But I heard absolutely nothing. Had they decided to put it off a day? I couldn't think why, though. It was either that or they were being so excruciatingly quiet that it was impossible for me to hear them. The ideas wrestled about in my mind, and in the end I just decided that enough thinking was enough. Putting my mind to rest, I curled up into a ball and let a deep sleep consume me.

~

The next morning, all was well and activity buzzed in the kitchen just like always. Anna greeted me cheerfully, breakfast simmering on the stove. Andrew and Jonathon came in from morning chores, and I suddenly realized I'd slept late again.

"Good morning," Andrew said, smiling.

Jonathon grinned at me with a flushed face.

Why were they acting this way? What about the slaves? Had they no interest in talking about the subject whatsoever? Well, I would bring it up. How dare they act as if nothing ever happened!

76

At breakfast, I pursed my lips and waited as Andrew and Anna chatted gaily over the weather. Pushing my food around in circles on my plate, I finally had enough.

"Ahem." I made an effort to clear my throat very loudly.

All conversation ceased and I was met with blank stares.

"Catherine?" Anna asked. "You have somethin' to say?"

I smiled in pleasure. "Yes, actually I do. What indeed happened with the . . . um . . . escape last night?"

"Oh!" Anna's face transformed into sudden realization. "They arrived safely across the Mississippi. All was well."

I nodded, stunned and unsatisfied expression on my face clearly readable. That's it? That was all she had to say? Well, apparently I was the only one extremely fascinated with the whole set-up. Or maybe they were all just used to it.

Picking up my fork, I shook my head in disappointment and began to eat. All that week, I couldn't breathe, think, sleep, or eat without imagining the hidden people that would live silently in the basement. It was scary, really, to think of it. Any moment, I imagined, a slave would accidentally reveal his place and the police would be knocking on our door, coming to arrest us. In my spare time at night, I would just sit on my bed and listen to the clock's ticking, trying to think how hard it must be for fugitives to be quiet all the time like that. When would the others come? What would they need? Food? Water? How did they know when it was safe for the slaves to leave? How did they know if a slave catcher resided in the city? All these questions and more drove me nearly mad. I knew none of it was for me to worry about, but in all truth, I was extremely curious. And it wasn't just that. I was interested in the Underground Railroad. It was all so new to me, so . . . real and enticing.

~

Sunday morning, I awoke to a sudden gust of cold wind and a sprinkle of rain. Scrambling to my feet, I quickly closed the open window. Shivering, I slipped on my heavy woolen robe. I peeked out my window, watching as an endless sheet of rain fell upon all as far as I could see. I watched as the horses and cows grazed as always in the fields, prancing around and enjoying the rainstorm. Actually, I did like it when it rained. I used to sit at my window and listen to the soft dribble of the raindrops, the loud echoing of thunder and the quick flashes of lightning. Silently, I breathed on the window, causing little puffs of white vapor to form on the glass. I traced a huge raindrop as it traveled down the window with my fingertip but flinched away at the coolness of the windowpane. The rain was always so calm, so breathtaking and peaceful. It made me just want to lie down again and curl up in bed, but instead, I yawned something furious and started to dress. Remembering my morning duties, I groaned and tugged on a ragged dress and my work boots. Hurrying downstairs, I saw that no one had awakened yet. Good. I had the house all to myself, and Jonathon wouldn't get to see me make a fool of myself.

Striding out into the fresh, morning air, I made my way to the barn. After grabbing a pail, I moved down the line of cows and surprisingly was able to milk all of them very well. Except Betsy, that is. Puffing a breath and pushing a strand of hair away from my forehead, I stooped down and carefully tugged on one of the udders. No reply. Good. Very good. Pulling a slight bit harder, Betsy's eyes widened and she scooted forward. Well, this was going to be harder than I thought. Without thinking, I began to sing a song. Surprisingly, the cow looked back at me with bug-eyes and moved back to where I sat. Smiling, I continued to sing.

"When Israel was in Egypt's land, let my people go. Oppressed so hard they could not stand, Let my people go . . ."

My voice coaxed the lunatic cow, and she gradually gave me lead to milk her without any harm done. After thanking her kindly, I shut the barn door and shuffled toward the chicken coop, yawning and gazing up into the light pink sky.

The chickens were even easier, for all I had to do was splash the feed down and watch them eat, scurrying around in all directions. They were hilarious to watch, actually, and their amusing natures made me want to sit and watch them for hours. Crazy creatures. Rubbing the back of my neck, I congratulated myself on a job well done and hurried back to the house.

Still, no one was awake, so I quietly crept up the stairs and made my way to my room, shutting the door behind me. A bubble of excitement surged through me as I remembered I would get to wear my new yellow skirt and blouse for church. During my normal routine of dressing, I heard the shuffling of feet as the family began to wake. After taking my time to make myself look presentable, I hurried downstairs. I danced into the kitchen and began to set the table.

"Cinnamon buns for breakfast!" Anna called over her shoulder.

Andrew was at his usual place, quite enveloped in the news article he read, and Jonathon was at the table also, all bright faced and as handsome as ever. After everything was ready, we all enjoyed some of Anna's warm cinnamon rolls.

Anticipation fluttered inside me. Sundays were exciting, as I got to see the "young people", as Anna put it.

~

I was eager to go to church, hoping I'd see Mallory again. She was such a sweet girl. But I dreaded Rosalie. I allowed thought to what Anna had said about all the boys being sweet on me. Of course I didn't believe it. Anyway, how would she know?

After our buggy came to a stop near the building, we all hurried inside, not wanting to get our Sunday's best wet for the church service. Once inside, we made our way to the pew, and I found Mallory at once. She was a couple rows behind me, and smiled broadly when she saw me. I waved back, glad to have a new friend. Looking around for the other girls, I spotted Rosalie enter the church doors with her family. She wore a stunning gown the shade of spring green, posing as quite a contrast with the weather. Flouncing down the aisle, she flashed a proud smile in everyone's direction. Looking to Mallory, I saw she wore the same aggravated face, and I stuck out my tongue so she'd know I felt the same about her. Mallory laughed and pointed toward the pulpit when the booming organ music began. Righting myself forward in my seat, I saw William, Rosalie's brother, staring intently at me, as if trying to gather everything he wanted to know about me all at once by staring me down. When our eyes met, he glanced away, most embarrassed.

When Pastor Dominic's powerful voice sounded out through the church, the congregation fell silent. Even though I had told myself in the past repeatedly God didn't care about me, I listened carefully to each and every word.

"You may be lost. You may be in such a predicament with no one to turn to. And friends, I tell you this: turn to God. He is the only one who can help you in your darkest days. Mere human troubles are no match for His almighty power.

"Please, don't doubt the Lord. Instead, let Him comfort you. Let Him pull you out of the dark and into the light. And as I mentioned before, have faith in him. Don't doubt what grand things He can do for you. Don't hide from Him because of pride. It says in Proverbs, 'Lean not on your own understanding'."

I let his words sink in, surprised that everything he said seemed dedicated to me. Maybe I could at least try to pray. I hadn't in a very long time, though. Would I still know how? And would God listen to me?

Yes. The word was a hushed whisper, so quiet in fact that I wondered if I really heard it. After church was over, I sat quietly in the pew, feeling the same overwhelming power I'd felt when I prayed with Milly a long time ago. Was He really listening? Yes, had been the simple answer. Why was believing it so difficult, though?

"Catherine Carey!" Mallory called, bustling over to me in her plaid skirts. "Such a beautiful day, don't you agree?"

I was amazed that she liked the rain. Most girls stuck up their noses at such weather, chatting gaily only on sunny weather, but sneering if it ever shone too brightly.

We stood together for a moment, and then Mallory brought up the subject of the husking bee.

"Oh, I'm sure it will be fun!" she cooed, taking my hand. "And it's tomorrow! I have so much to do! I still haven't found something nice to wear."

"Mallory?" I asked gravely, changing the subject to a more serious one as my eyes drifted over to the group of young men.

"Yes?"

"What do you know of William Andrews?'

"Oh! He and Jonathon are best friends. They are . . . what shall I say? Quite popular with the young ladies? Does that sound right?"

I laughed. "Is that true?"

"Oh, yes. All the girls practically are breaking their hearts between the two. Why do you ask?"

"I caught William looking at me several times today."

Mallory gasped. "He's smitten with you probably!"

"You think so?"

"Oh, yes." Mallory paused for a moment. "But what of Jonathon?"

"What about him?" I asked in a hushed tone.

"Oh, please. You must catch him watching you, too? Also, you live with him! How is that?"

"It's . . . fine." I thought a minute, remembering all the times I found his gaze lingering on my face.

"Then take your pick." She said the words with such enthusiasm I laughed out loud. Before another word was said, William strode over to me. My breath caught in my throat, and I couldn't make eye contact with him.

"Miss Carey?"

I nodded, quite aware of all the eyes on William and me, including Jonathon's.

"Would you be so kind as to let me stay close to you at the husking bee tomorrow?" His green eyes pleaded with so much uncertainty that it would almost be a crime to turn him down.

"All right," I said, swallowing a gulp of ambiguity.

His face beamed. "Good. I will see you there, then?"

I nodded, brushing back a stray curl.

He smiled with new confidence before re-joining his group. Several young men smiled wryly at him, others laughed out loud. But Jonathon's face was unlike anything

I'd ever seen before. It was pure jealousy. That I was sure of!

~

That night, for some reason, I had an amazing, wonderful, terrible nightmare. Yes, that's what I mean. Jonathon was close to me, and I swear I could almost taste the familiar, delicious fragrance of him. And then he kissed me, just perfectly on the mouth. Part of me was screaming, and the other part was relaxing. The screaming side of me won, so I forced open my eyes and sat up to find myself actually yelling at the top of my lungs. Oh, no. Covering a hand over my persisting holler, I plunged back under the covers and shut my eyes, hoping no one had heard my sudden outburst. What would Anna say? I know.

She'd say, "Did you have a bad dream?"

And I'd say, "Yes!"

Then Anna would ask, "What was it about, darlin'?"

And I'd reply, "Well, in my dream your son, Jonathon, was kissing me right on the lips and I was enjoying it while I was hating it."

Well, I most certainly wasn't going to confess that. So I just hoped they hadn't heard. After a moment of listening for a rustle or a movement, I confirmed the undisturbed silence. But no matter how hard I tried, how long I lay there, I couldn't possibly sleep. And then, it was twelve o'clock. I know because the millions and billions of clocks chimed away, ringing and making all sorts of racket. But there was another sound, too. Hushed whispers and the soft patter of feet. Then I knew. The Walters and I were not alone; we had company. In that split second I plunged out of bed, not caring to look in the mirror. I carefully crept down the stairs, and what I saw at the doorway didn't surprise me. Taking a seat on one of the stairs, I tried to hide myself from view.

I couldn't make out everything that was said, but I saw that the front door was cracked open slightly and Anna was whispering to the unknown fugitives on the other side.

"Who's there?" she asked quietly.

A pause heavy enough to rattle one's brain.

"A friend," whispered a man's husky voice, "with friends."

I stifled a gasp and watched intently as twelve dark-skinned, flustered and disheveled Negroes shuffled across the doorstep. They were shivering, despite the mild night. Two dozen frightened eyes peeked out from solemn, silent faces. No one spoke. No one moved. One woman clutched protectively on to her child, a boy no older than four or five. The fact that a child so small would join the group surprised me. Six middle-aged men with determined yet stone-still faces accompanied the group of fugitives, along with four women and two children, including the small boy. They all stood perfectly still, not sacrificing one movement. I couldn't even make out the heaving of a chest from breathing. Were they breathing? Were they even there?

Suddenly, I felt a hand brush my bare shoulder. Stifling a gasp, my heart caught in my throat. Jonathon sat dangerously near to me, blue eyes open wide.

"Why are you up?" he asked in a voice so quiet my ears had to strain to hear.

"I . . . well, I just," I was at a loss for words, and I couldn't keep my voice as quiet as his. "Well, I was curious, and—"

Apparently I was talking too loud, for Jonathon shook his head and put a finger to my moving lips. Shivers ran up my spine, and I closed my mouth. He turned his attention back to the scene downstairs, and I practically had to tear my eyes away from him to do the same.

"You must have had a hard journey. Come with me. Let's get something—" Anna broke the never ending silence.

"Ma'am," one tall man said, stepping forward, "we thank you for your hospitality. But we ain't stayin' too late tonight. Could we please just have a meal? We in a rush to get across the Mississippi."

"Oh, of course. I'll have my husband accompany you—"

"No." The man shook his head. "That ain't necessary since we know the way already. Moses be waitin' for us tonight acrost the river. But thank you anyways. We'll have a meal and be off."

His deep voice and huge, muscled body intimidated me. I cowered back, and found myself leaning into Jonathon's chest. To my surprise, he didn't slink away, instead holding onto me with a firm grip. He obviously understood my state of shock.

"That's just fine," Anna said gravely. "Please, follow me."

Anna led the slaves away to the kitchen. I sat still, deafening heartbeat absorbing all the other conversation I might have heard. Jonathon's grip on my elbow lightened slightly, and I breathed out heavily. Having him near me did my wildly beating heart no good at all.

"Well, I guess I won't be needing to lead them away," Jonathon said, staring blankly into space.

I nodded solemnly, biting my lip. Now what?

"We best be getting some sleep," Jonathon stated, rising to his feet and pulling me with him.

My heart raced as his gaze roamed over me, finally deciding to rest on my face. Glancing away nervously, I shifted on my feet. Jonathon rubbed his eyes.

"Well, good night, Catherine."

I nodded, watching as he moved back into his room, shutting the door quietly behind him.

~

I don't know how long I lay there, face to the ceiling, waiting for the sleep that never came. After dozing off once or twice, eyes shooting open every so often, I groaned aloud and shoved back the covers, standing up. The slaves were gone, that I was positive of. Suddenly, in the middle of my yawn, my heart skipped a beat. As sleep evaded me, I had a sudden urge to play the piano. And if all those clocks didn't wake those slug-a-beds up, the piano certainly wouldn't. Tip-toeing on the soft carpet that squeaked in some places, I slowly made my way down the stairs and into the living room.

"What shall I play today?" I whispered to myself, arranging the pillow on the bench until I was comfortably positioned.

I let my fingers decide, and they chose "Ave Maria". It was also a very nice piece, slow and calming. Maybe it would help me sleep. I played softly though, minding the three sleeping people upstairs. When I had played the first time for the Walters, my eyes were suddenly opened to what great talent I had. My long fingers slid up and down the keys like magic, the notes forming a masterpiece. But between drawing and piano, I couldn't choose a favorite. They were both so dear to me. Yet, the piano I really *had*. Meaning, I knew I could play it any time, any song I wanted, well enough. But with my sketches, I was limited. I could only draw from sight, and honestly, I didn't know whether I was actually all that good or not. Also, I was also too shy to ask any one of the Walters to sit down and let me draw them, as the only person I wasn't afraid to draw in front of was Milly. What if they didn't like how I drew? I knew I was good at piano, but was I really all that wonderful with drawing? I surely thought I was, but did the slaves back home just praise me because I was the daughter of the man who owned them? Well, maybe someday I'd reveal my sketches to the world, but for now I'd rather just keep them to myself, drawing only nature's beauty and the things around me. Portraits were extremely tempting, though, and I longed to draw another besides Milly.

After the song, I couldn't tell you how long I sat staring into space, thinking about everything under the sun. I thought of my terrible, wonderful dream. I started when I heard the steps' creaking sound. Shooting up from the piano bench and whirling around, I saw Jonathon walk toward me, rubbing his eyes with the heels of his hands. His black hair was tousled, and he wore sleeping trousers and a white nightshirt.

"What are you doing up?" he asked in a slow, sleep-filled voice.

I didn't know how to answer. "I couldn't get to sleep."

Surprisingly, he just stared at me for a moment. "Me neither."

I blew out a sigh of relief. We both just stood there for an awkward moment, looking at each other, and then, at the same time, our feet led us to separate chairs. I curled up, tucking my chin to my knees, my legs glued to my chest. I was only wearing a morning robe and a nightdress, but really, what did it matter? I'd seen Jonathon before in my nightclothes. And besides, the proper society rules didn't even seem to apply here. Suddenly, I could see Jonathon staring at me from the corner of my eye. I looked to him, and he quickly averted his gaze.

"Want to see the sunrise?" he asked, catching me off guard.

I merely nodded, following him out to the porch. We sat together on the wooden swing, close, but not too close. I was thankful for that. My heart started to beat faster, as it had been doing lately when I was around him, and I tried with all my might to calm it. Hot sensations ran all through my body, and even though the morning was cool and crisp, I was as warm as a burning stove. Did he expect me to make conversation? I certainly would not, if that's what he was thinking. It was his idea to come out here anyway. But before I could stop, the urge to ask the question I'd been dying to escaped from my mouth.

"Do you miss your sister?" After the horrible words came out, I bit my tongue.

He hesitated, then looked at the sun peeking slightly over the horizon and nodded. "How'd you find out about her?"

"Your mother told me. Forgive me for saying anything. I know it still hurts," I apologized, gazing at the beautiful, yellow-orange ball that rose slowly up into the smeary, blue sky. Oh, if only I had my sketch book . . . .

"She would be about your age now if she were still alive. And don't say you're sorry. Maybe it'd do me good to talk about it." He turned his eyes to me, and I saw compassion mixed with glints of sadness in their blue depths.

"What did she look like?"

"She had dark, wavy hair, like me, and eyes as blue as the Pacific itself."

"Like yours," I whispered, and then quickly scolded myself for doing so. What a thing to say!

He grinned, looking at me. Oh, how handsome he was!

"She was tall and strong, and she was so humorous," he chuckled, probably picturing her laugh. "She could turn the oddest situation into a joke. I loved her so much."

I didn't want to probe any longer, so I fell silent.

"And then . . . we went ice-skating one day. On that lake down there. And she fell in, and I couldn't . . . I didn't save her. I hate myself for that."

He thought it was his fault! How could he! Without thinking, I placed a hand on his arm, and when he flinched at my touch, I pulled away.

"It's not your fault. You did nothing wrong. Things just happen," I soothed, thinking of the fire that destroyed my home. *Life goes on . . . life goes on . . . life goes on . . .*

The ruthless words rang through my head, and suddenly, I didn't believe in them like I used to. They were totally careless and dispassionate.

"But I could have tried to help her . . ." he argued, and I could tell he was fighting inner battles. I wanted to make him feel better, to grab all his stress and bunch it into a ball and throw it into the chicken coop. Better yet, I wanted to kiss him. And not just a tiny kiss, a long, deep one. I wanted all his harsh feelings to go away. The thought of it scared me, and I inched a little away from him. I couldn't be thinking those things.

"Anyway, I have chores to start," he finally said, moving to stand up.

"Jonathon," I whispered. "It's not your fault. Remember that."

Nodding warily, he stood up. And without another word, we both departed.

~

I had forgotten that it was William who was escorting me to the husking bee. Frankly, I had forgotten all about the husking bee. The Walters were already outside chopping down the rest of the corn. How could I have been so stupid as to forget something so important? Well, I'd go outside at least and try to help them. My heart thumped faster as I pulled on my boots. Outside, I saw many black servants helping Jonathon and Andrew with the corn. A horse-drawn contraption boarded several men and magically cut down the stalks of corn, making a huge pile on the back of the wagon.

"Anna?" I called to her. She was talking with several servant women.

"Oh, hello dear!" she chirped excitedly when she saw me. "Might I introduce you to Nina and Mama Mabel? This is Catherine."

I remembered Nina as the mother of the little girl and baby boy. Mama Mable I'd never seen before. She was short and awfully chubby and was probably in her late fifties. She wore a huge, floppy straw hat with roses and tiny leaves sewn into it. Her face was smudged with wrinkles, and she didn't look much like the happy type.

"I know you, Catherine. We met before." Nina said, patting my shoulder.

Mama Mable said nothing, a grumpy expression on her face. I wondered why Anna referred to her as "Mama." Oh, well. I needn't concern myself over it.

"She has a beau already! William Andrews is takin' her to the huskin' bee tonight!" Anna gloated, smiling from ear to ear. "I just knew he was sweet on her."

"Well, this job looks about done. Who's with me for somethin' cold to drink?"

"I betta not. Maureen is waitin' at the house with them babies. She good with children, but I don't believe anyone can be too good with mine," explained Nina. And with that, she bid us farewell and trudged back to her cabin.

Mama Mable stared at me for a moment, then nodded to Anna and agreed, "Somethin' to drink."

So all three of us strolled back to the house, Anna and Mama Mable exchanging a few words back and forth. I could also tell Mable wasn't exactly the talkative type that Anna was. I almost giggled at how the two could be friends. But it was strange how Anna could actually be *good friends* with her servants. Papa had barely acknowledged their presences.

During our little "tea party", I learned that Mama Mable was the baby-sitter of the bunch. She and a teenage girl they called Maureen watched the children while the women and men worked during the daytime. Since Mama Mable was getting older, Maureen would take over the job when the former couldn't handle it anymore. Despite her being unfriendly and straight faced, I liked the old woman. She made me want to laugh out loud, I daresay. It's not that I was cruel; it's just that she was a funny little woman.

I was also interested in Maureen, the servant girl, because I'd never seen another girl my age on the farm.

After Mable left and the men were back in the house, Anna said it was time for cooking. She and I were to prepare fried chicken. Everyone else attending would bring a dish. That day, Andrew went out into the chicken coop to fetch a chicken for Anna to cook. I grimaced and hid my face inside while Jonathon teased me non-stop, watching the scene as if a joyous parade was going by. Anna shooed the men away and hid the chicken from my sight after it was plucked. I couldn't bear the thought that I had just fed the poor little creature.

While the chicken roasted in the oven, Anna and I decided to work on some mending.

"Anna?" I asked once we settled down in the living room with the clothes.

"Mmhmmm?"

"Is there a secret passage way? You know, to get to the cellar?"

"You're sitting on top of it." She peered up at me with a mysterious grin.

I looked all around me but found that I sat over nothing but an innocent wooden floor and a rug.

"You just have to lift up that rug. There's a door."

I smiled. "So if there is a slave catcher in town, what do you do if you have slaves hidden?"

"Well, if one is prowlin' around this part of town, we have to wait to hear from certain sources when it's safe to plan to leave. We can't just all high-tail it down the road and not expect to get ourselves in boilin' water. Usually, though, we always get our fugitives safe across the Mississippi that very night. We only put them in the cellar when we know they have to stay the night—when it's unsafe for them to travel any further."

I treaded outside after I helped a little with the mending, and to my surprise, the outdoors was a hive of busy people swarming all around setting up tables and stacking corn. Since I didn't want to be in the way, I took a stroll into the fields that were now bare, except for the occasional spare stalk or lone piece of corn. Something caught my eye as I headed forward. There on the ground, face down, lay little Lacy's rag doll. I decided to return it with her; it gave me a reason to venture away from all the hustle and bustle, anyway.

Approaching the log cabin, I observed that about five or six young children were playing in the grassy yards. It didn't take long to locate Lacy, for she was being chased by another little girl, both of them hollering at the top of their lungs. The girl whom I supposed was Maureen yelled at them to hush when I stepped forward.

"Hello," I said cheerfully, looking straight at Maureen. She was about my height, with a pretty face and light bronze skin. Her eyes were strangely colored, not brown or black, but dark gray. A beautiful color. Never in my life had I seen a Negro with eyes that color—like silver.

Maureen smiled sourly then scooped up Lacy, whispering to her. I wondered what made this girl so bitter and prim. She wore a low, curly ponytail, and her blue apron was dirty and worn.

Immediately, Lacy jumped out of Maureen's arms and raced toward me, yelling my name.

"Oh! Cafrine, you found her! You found my Angela!"

"I thought you'd like her back," I said, handing her the doll.

She grasped her tight, pulling the little doll close to her chest. "Oh, thank you! Thank you! I must've left 'er in the fields."

"Well, be careful next time you're playing or the dolly monster will eat her up!" I teased.

Lacy giggled before running off again.

I tried another glance at the girl to find her eyes intently on me, studying me. I smiled, and she averted her eyes.

"You must be Maureen," I ventured, and she nodded slightly. "I'm Catherine Carey; the Walters are my godparents, and I'm living with them now, as you may have heard."

She blinked and turned her attention back to the children. She didn't care one thing about me. I was merely a speck in her eye, a hindrance and an annoyance. I knew this was a sign she wanted nothing to do with me, so I said goodbye to Lacy and left, a little discouraged.

~

93

Later that day, I was unexpectedly without a thing to do. And then I thought of Lacy's old doll. Surely I could put together something better than that. I most certainly could sew a doll, even though my sewing wasn't the best around. I opened my bureau drawer and pulled out my needle and thread. Then I chose some peach fabric for the skin from the needlework basket Anna had given me. But I caught my mistake, hurriedly replacing the peach for the brown. I then cut out two identical shapes of a girl's body in the fabric before lacing the needle and thread. After that, I began to sew the two pieces of the body together, carefully trying to make each stitch small and careful.

"The smaller the stitch, the better," Miss Montgomery had always advised.

Even though I had never been the best at sewing, I was extremely proud of my job when the doll was near complete. I decided dry beans would work best for stuffing. Creeping downstairs, I was greatly relieved when I saw Anna outside talking with her husband. I filed through the kitchen pantry, searching for dried beans. There was a spare can at the bottom containing some old rice. That would do.

After stuffing the doll and sewing up the last part, I carefully traced some lines on the doll's face lightly with a pencil. Then, with my ink pen, I traced the lines to make them dark, making each line precise and thin. I made the eyes almond shaped and big, the lips full and dark, and the nose small and round, like a button. Then I added eyelashes and thin lines for eyebrows. For clothes, I tore off a little piece of a laced petticoat I'd purchased in Charleston and tied it around the doll's body as a dress.

"There now!" I exclaimed, looking my doll over. Only then did I notice she had no hair. Blast, I had no yarn.

Again, I descended the staircase, in search for yarn. I found in the piano bench a bag full of fabric and yarn. After returning to my room, I decided the doll should have long hair. I cut the right amount and sewed it into the head, making sure each piece lay perfectly framed around the face. After the doll was complete, I observed her, beaming with triumph.

I decided to give the doll to Lacy in the morrow. I couldn't contain my happiness as I thought of what her face would look like when she would see it. Oh, and I wanted her to like it. I hid the tiny doll in my top drawer, placing her in carefully before closing it. Hopefully Lacy would be more cautious with this doll. I smiled at the thought, and then realized with alarm how much time I had taken on this project. How I let time just slip away! I took a fleeting glance at my clock. I only had twenty minutes until the corn husking! And I wasn't even ready!

Quickly, I pulled on a new blue skirt that Anna had sewn for me and placed in my bureau as a surprise. I was beginning to like it better than the yellow one. Then I slipped on the new white blouse and some of my walking boots. I carelessly threw some color on my face and loosely braided my hair down my back, a style I'd seen a girl wear in church. A sudden outburst of bubbly, luring laughter drifted from outdoors, and it made my heart soar with anticipation. I took no more time. By the next minute, I was outside joining the last-minute preparations for the husking bee.

~

My heart stopped when Jonathon came out, starched shirt and navy overalls fresh and clean. His hair was tousled slightly, curling, and his eyes were already bright with evident merriment. My heart resumed beating regularly but was nonetheless excited when more people began to arrive, including William. I couldn't help but dread William's presence. It's not that I didn't like him; he seemed all right. But honestly I didn't want to be *his* date. I saw his gaze search the crowd for me, but I slinked far away, hoping the people congregating around me would act as my shield. In a moment, I found my back against a tree. I realized at that moment I wasn't just hiding from William, I was hiding from the crowd as a whole. I was actually *shy*. I knew hiding would solve nothing, but I just couldn't face everyone.

It seemed so sudden, how the once empty yard had transformed into a bustling cluster of laughing, cheery people. Silently deep in thought, I was taken by the shoulders and shook slightly.

"Catherine! Whatever are you doing behind a tree? William and I have looked all over for you! Come on, your godfather is going to make a speech now. Come on!" Mallory grabbed my hand and led me to a place in front of the wooden platform where Andrew stood smiling. Laura and May were there, and William, clad in his Sunday's best, came and stood next to me. When I turned to him, overwhelmed, he smiled broadly, and I saw a red blush flood his cheeks.

"Friends," Andrew boomed, trying to hush the noisy mob.

After a minute, everything was still and my heart thumped wildly in my chest. I scanned the many faces around me, eyes abruptly landing on Rosalie's perfect, animated face. Her lips were edged with a self-satisfied smirk, and her naughty blue eyes were focused on someone or something, but who or what? I followed her direct gaze right to the back of Jonathon's head. A pang of anger and jealousy shot through me. Andrew's thunderous voice brought me back down to earth.

"Welcome, everyone. We thank you all for coming out this evening. Why, it's always nice to see all of our good neighbors together. Now let us just all have a good time and thank the Lord for bringing us all together—"

"Oh, Andrew!" I heard Anna scold, jumping up on the wooden platform. She gave her husband a playful shove, urging him to step down. A wave of laughter erupted from the audience. "For goodness sakes, Andrew, they'll all die from boredom before you finish your speech. Everyone, first we'll do they huskin', and then we'll move on to a little dinner that the ladies have made. And then a little bit of dancing I suppose wouldn't hurt. I think some of the men have brought their instruments, right Bill? Yes? Good."

Cheers of eagerness evaporated from the crowd, and soon the fiddler struck up a merry tune while the people moved toward the piles of corn. Instantly, I felt a twinge of joy. Anticipation swelled inside me, causing the knot of fear to slowly loosen. William remained by my side, making occasional small talk as we each grabbed an ear of corn. Laura, May, and Mallory chatted gaily by my side, and I secretly wished that, like them, I had come to the bee as a single lady.

"Why, everyone knows if you get the red ear you get a kiss," Mallory chirped. "And we all know who William is going to claim if he gets the red ear!"

I blushed and looked away.

I heard Rosalie's voice and turned to see her making her way toward us. I squared my jaw and clenched my teeth, forcing myself to smile.

"Why, hello ladies. How is the night finding you?" she asked with a toss of her curls.

"Oh, just fine," I retorted with the same false jollity. "And you?"

"Quite well, actually." Rosalie purposely gazed at Jonathon with these words, and I ripped harder on my piece of corn.

A moment later, Rosalie's excited yells rose above the crowd.

"I've got it!" she bellowed. "I've got a red ear of corn!"

Gritting my teeth, I watched as everyone around her watched expectantly.

"I get a kiss from . . ." She turned right to Jonathon, and I grimaced. His face turned bright pink, but before I could really read his expression, Rosalie threw her arms around him and planted a kiss right on his lips. After she pulled away, I could see the accomplished look on her face and hear the hoots of the boys around Jonathon. She hung her arms sumptuously around his neck, her curls bobbing around every which way as she smiled at those around her. I turned my attention away from the sight. I hope Andrew had seen that disgusting display. Glancing about, I caught sight of him. He stood laughing with some of his old friends. I grimaced; I was the only one that felt uncomfortable by Rosalie's revolting behavior, apparently.

I followed William to the food table, and my mouth nearly drooled at the wonders I saw. Vanilla iced cakes, plump fruit-filled pies, and steamy casseroles, among other dishes, smothered the table. I wouldn't have been surprised if the table buckled in half under such a load. Oh, and how my belly groaned for a taste of everything! I didn't want to take too much, so I spooned appropriate servings onto my plate. Once I took my seat beside William on one of the wooden benches, he struck up a business-related conversation with me, and I became quickly irritated. Ladies were never supposed to talk about business and such with men, and although I'd abandoned mostly all of the rules Miss Mortemeyer had taught me, this was one rule I intended on sticking to.

"And we own that factory you know. That one downtown. And of course, I'm going to inherit that . . . ." He went on and on, and I wearily responded with nods of my head and weak, half-hearted smiles.

I observed Jonathon, then, for a minute, as William continued. Mallory had informed me the girls adored him, but as I watched him, he did nothing to encourage them. Several girls took the initiative to start conversation with him, but he seemed bent on remaining quiet, fading into the background, and offering little effort to conversation at hand. Was he really that shy? Or was he just disinterested? I couldn't decide.

A shrill scream pierced the happy atmosphere, silencing the crowd. I turned to see Rosalie standing by the privy, a small, dark figure cowering beside her.

"What are *you* doing here?" Rosalie hollered.

Lacy. I bounded over to the small child, and in one simple sweep she was in my protective arms, tear-filled face buried in my chest. I became furious. Suddenly every pair of eyes was on the scene. Gasps and wide-eyed stares found their way to Lacy and me.

"Catherine!" Rosalie looked appalled. "Set her down at once! She was trying to sneak her way into the privy when I was in there! Wretched child."

I put Lacy down, and she clung to my skirts. I felt like striking Rosalie, but instead I controlled my anger and composed myself like a lady.

"Never call her such a name again," I said coolly. "I'm sure she hadn't been trying to peek in on you, either. Now look what you have done. You have successfully diverted all the attention to yourself at the cost of this little girl's disposition. I'm sure you are very satisfied with yourself, as always."

And with that, I grabbed Lacy in my arms and strode away, leaving the gaping people behind. I meant what I said, and I didn't regret one word. It's about time Rosalie got what she deserved. Slowing my pace once we were far away, I stroked Lacy's hair and whispered soothing words to her, just as Milly did for me on the day of the fire.

"Ca-afrine . . ." she choked on her sobbing words. "I don't li-ike her. She-es me-ean."

"I know it," I said. "But you're going home now. What were you doing up so late anyway? That was a long walk to make alone at such an hour. Well, it doesn't matter now. Do not say a word of this night to anyone. If you do, I'll have to explain the whole thing to your mother. Agreed?"

I felt her nod against my shoulder, and I held her tighter.

The cabin was dark, so Lacy crept through the back door. Her mother and father were already asleep, it seemed.

"You can make it from here?" I asked her.

"Yes, ma'am." She brushed away her tears. "I'm almost five."

I would have laughed aloud if I hadn't been near a house filled with sleeping people.

"All right. Good night, Lacy," I said.

"Ni-night, Cafrine. Thank you for saving me.

~

When I arrived upon the husking bee, the crowd was tense, no doubt bewildered at the event that had just taken place. I regretted coming back, but before I could have a chance to run inside, Mallory and Anna rushed to me, asking if I was all right.

"Of course I am," I assured them.

Anna took me in her arms, and Mallory grasped my hand.

"Where is poor Lacy?" Anna asked, pulling back.

"She's safe in bed. What about Rosalie? Where is she?"

Mallory snorted. "She and her family left minutes ago. You should have seen William! His face like a corpse's! Oh, for Pete's sake, Catherine! I don't know what to think. I'm mighty proud of you, but you really caught everyone off guard. Especially Rosalie! No one has ever spoken up to her! What a day! I bet you she's crying right now!"

"Well, Mallory. That's her business, child," Anna gently rebuked.

Mallory sighed. "Yes, I suppose."

"Girls, let's go back to the party now. We must all forget this."

"Yes," Mallory and I agreed in unison.

"Good. Come along, then."

A few pairs of eyes glanced my way, but for the most part, it was as if nothing even happened. I was a little relieved William and Rosalie were gone. Except the moment I caught Jonathon's puzzled eyes on me, I blushed and the queasy knot inside my stomach tightened once again. But this time, for the first time, he didn't look away. He just kept on looking at me, as if his eyes were asking me a question, patiently waiting for an answer. I decided to ignore him, joining in the conversation with Mallory and the girls, who all congratulated me on my "act of bravery." Honestly, I had no idea what they were talking about. If they had been in my shoes, they would have done the same thing. Right? My thoughts were disrupted when a shadow loomed over me. Jonathon. Looking up, I saw him smile slightly, wearing the same expression that he wore the time he discovered I could play the piano. I couldn't help myself. I smiled back. My heart thumped faster as he reached out his hand to me.

"Would you care to dance?" he asked. If he was nervous, he did a pretty fine job of hiding it. I, on the other hand, trembled all over when he took my hand. All I could do was stare at him through wide eyes. I was in a daze as he led me to a vacant place in the yard.

"This is gonna be a fast song," Jonathon smiled.

Fast song? I'd rather not. But his friendly grin was so tempting, and his blue eyes were so beautiful, and the night was so perfect, and the moon and the stars looked so nice that I just went along with it.

"Ready?" asked Jonathon.

My heart screamed yes, but my mind screamed no. I hesitated, but Jonathon placed a large warm hand around my waist, pulling me just a little closer. The fiddler broke into a lively chorus and the other musicians joined in. My breath was knocked out of me as he inched me closer to him, his other hand tightening on mine. Sensations I'd never felt before spiraled through me, sending bursts of feelings in all directions.

"But, I don't know how to dance like . . . like this. I really don't—" I tried to protest, but Jonathon just shook his head and laughed that deep, joyous laugh of his. My knees felt like jelly, and I wanted to swoon right then and there so I wouldn't have to go through with this. My mind whirled around in circles, and I was completely breathless in his arms as he swung me around the whole yard. Hoots and laughter drifted to my ears, and that combined with Jonathon's laughing must have loosened up my nerves, for a bubbly giggle escaped my mouth.

I loved the way dark night surrounded us. I loved the smell of the evening air and the way the stars looked.

I loved the laughs about me, the cheers and the excited voices. I loved the music, and everything else. And for a moment, I saw something in Jonathon's eyes . . . something I'd never planned on seeing. And right then, I forgot about everything that had ever happened to me. I forgot about my parents, and the fire, and South Carolina. It seemed I had always been just like this—here with Jonathon—and we'd just always been dancing and smiling. Jonathon had always had that look in his beautiful eyes.

And then, the fiddler's song stopped, and both of us stood there, Jonathon's hand lingering just a little too long on my waist. His smile faded, and for a split second I though he was going to kiss me. My first *real* kiss. I trembled at the thought, and Jonathon must have noticed.

"Are you okay? You're shivering. Are you cold?" He took my hand and led me over to a bench where no one else loitered.

Cold? Not with you. "I'm fine. Just a little tired is all." I smoothed out every crease in my skirts, itching for a distraction. My heartbeat soared and I suddenly felt all nervous again. Was this how I would always feel around Jonathon? What was wrong with me? If that's what love felt like, I didn't like it. Or did I? My thoughts were muddled, and I pleaded with my heart for reconciliation.

It was quiet for a moment between us, and I tried with all my might to block out every person around us, and just close in on Jonathon and hear his slow breathing, listen to his rhythmic heartbeat. But I could do neither of those things. Not now. Not here.

"I'm proud of you for standing up for Lacy. It takes a lot of courage to do something like that," Jonathon praised in a soft tone of voice. I wanted to reach out to him, better yet kiss him, but I couldn't . . . wouldn't do that. Was it the night that caused these sudden urges? The music? The mood? I didn't know, and I shuddered.

"Lacy didn't deserve to be treated like . . ."

"Like a Negro?" Jonathon finished my sentence, catching me off guard.

He studied me intently, and his eyes shone like the stars in the velvety night sky. His black waves glistened with the moonlight, and I swear he never looked more handsome. And his jaw wasn't clenched or angry. It had a new, tender bend to it. And just when I was about to die of heartbreak, Anna's voice rang through the air loud and clear.

"All right, everybody! Let's wrap up the night with one last song! How about it, boys?" She turned to the band, who smiled wryly from underneath bristly beards. And then the fiddle struck up another tune, but neither Jonathon nor I responded at all. We just remained gazing into each other's eyes, not really knowing if this all was a dream or not. But soon, too soon actually, everyone started to leave and say goodbye. It was sad, actually, that the night ended so soon. But I was grateful for the quiet now. If only he'd kissed me . . .

I scolded myself for thinking such things, and I wearily helped the family clean every last crumble of dirt up as my punishment.

"Did you have fun, darlin'?" Anna asked as we made our way upstairs to retire for the night.

Oh, yes. More than you could imagine. "Yes, very much so. What about you?"

"Oh," she said, "I always do. Well, sweet dreams."

"Thank you. Good night."

And just before I dozed off that night in bed, I must have replayed the time spent with Jonathon about a thousand times. I couldn't forget his smell, the dimpled smile, and the way his eyes could light up . . .

~

The next morning, my heart was solemnly set on giving the doll to Lacy. So after my morning chores I bounded over the hills, chilly air slicing into my skin. I briskly paced to Lacy's home, where I saw a continuous puff of gray smoke rise and curl up into the air. The little cottage was quiet and peaceful, and I expected Lacy to jump outside greeting me at any minute. Knocking three times on the door, I waited patiently until Nathaniel opened it.

"G'morning, Missy Catherine," he said cheerfully. *Missy Catherine.* That was what all my slaves had called me.

"Good morning, Nathaniel. Is Lacy home? I have something for her."

In a second, Lacy was by my feet, arms impulsively wrapped around my legs. She was still in her nightdress, her hair wild and tangled. I laughed out loud, and then bent down by her. I looked up once at the door to see Nathaniel and Nina watching me with joy filled to the brim in their eyes.

"I have a surprise for you," I whispered as if it were a secret.

"You do?" she whispered back.

I nodded, pulling the doll out from behind my back. Lacy squealed with happiness and grabbed the doll from my hands. Then, more carefully, she felt the pretty, soft fabric of the doll's dress and fingered the long, dark hair. She looked up at me, and I found tears hidden in their depths. It was surprising, finding tears in a little girl's eyes over getting such a simple gift, but I realized maybe Lacy didn't receive gifts all that often, that she wasn't like me. No one said a word, but in that moment of silence I sensed a new peace and respect between us all. I looked up to Nathaniel and Nina to find them smiling at me, tears streaming down Nina's face, awe evident on Nathaniel's. I felt as though they both saw me as something more than just a little, rich white girl. I was different in a way. Looking up into Lacy's eyes, I saw something else. Something similar to what I saw in my father's eyes long ago. Love. It was purely love. And before I could put another thought to it, Lacy was in my arms, hugging the life out of me. Returning the embrace, I heard Lacy whisper,

"Thank you, Cafrine." She looked up into my eyes and blinked, and my heart melted.

~

On my way back home, I was so jubilant that I was oblivious to the sound of a girl's scream coming from behind me. But finally my senses thawed, and I listened carefully to the sound. Spinning on my heel, I dashed as fast as I could to where the echoing shrill was coming from. And then I saw. Right over the grassy hill overlooking the spring, Maureen was sprawled out on the ground, ankle caught in a stern hole in the ground. When she saw me, she wailed harder, calling for help.

I responded by planting myself at her feet, trying to sum up the situation. Working with amazing pace, I slowly grooved the foot free, gently and quickly. She whimpered a little, but after a couple heartbeats, her foot was free. She couldn't move it though, and I knew at once it was badly hurt. Already a purple welt swelled painfully on it, about the size of half of a fist.

"Wait here," I told her. As if she could actually go anyplace. "I'll go get help. Hold on."

I sprinted up the hill and through the bare cornfields, utterly tense and my heart beating wildly. Finding Jonathon

106

by the barn, I grabbed his arm, trying to explain my story but failing to do so, as I was completely out of breath.

"Help!" I exclaimed, exasperated. "Come on! Maureen is hurt!"

Immediately Jonathon sprang into action. With swift motions, he threw together an ice pack and a binding cloth. In a moment, he and I were racing to the rescue. While Jonathon wound the cloth tightly around her ankle, I grasped her hand, which was damp with sweat, and with trusting eyes she looked into mine. My eyes must have seemed to say, *You'll be all right.* And hers seemed to reply, *I know. I trust you.* It was extraordinary, the bond that was strengthened between us in those moments. I was thankful that Jonathon worked so quickly, for I could only imagine what terrible pain poor Maureen was in. Together, we all made our way slowly back to Maureen's cabin. Between Jonathon and me, she was quite taken care of.

"That's my house." Maureen grunted and pointed to one of the cabins. The front door suddenly burst open and Mama Mable rushed out, puffing and muttering under her breath.

"Maureen!" she yelled. "What happened?"

Before she or I could respond, Jonathon said, "It looks like she might have a broken ankle!"

"Oh!" Mama Mable gasped, rushing over to us. "Come on and bring 'er inside. Put her in the bed."

The woman scurried back inside, propping the door wide open so we could all make it through. We laid Maureen gently on the bed, and she let out a sigh of relief at the comfort of it. Jonathon and I just stood there for a second, staring at Maureen, until she looked at us and whispered hoarsely,

"Thank you."

And then Mama Mable pushed us out, mumbling something about young folks and the pickles they get themselves into.

~

That afternoon, Anna told me to take over the cakes and cookies and pies left from the husking bee the night before. She said she'd be tempted to eat them all, and then she'd barely be able to fit through the door. I jumped at the opportunity, hoping to see Maureen again and confirm her new respect for me. I also wanted to see Lacy and her family, wanting to know how she liked her new doll so far. So I wrapped up as many goodies as I could and placed them in a basket, then slipped on a cape and hurried over to the servant's quarters. Lacy, Toby, and several other children ran around outside, while several adults conversed and raked golden-brown leaves that had just fallen off the trees. I realized then with a prick of delight that autumn was officially beginning. I truly loved the crisp, chilly weather, and I really adored all the beautiful trees. Glancing up to the distant hills, I suddenly noticed the glorious color around me. It had happened just overnight, seemingly. For the trees were luminous golds and magnificent oranges and vibrant reds. My, what beautiful trees Missouri had!

There certainly was a bountiful amount of desserts left over, and Anna told me to split everything as evenly as possible. There were eight cabins in all, and doing a quick sum in my head, I found that each household should receive two items. Many servants were out working with Andrew and Jonathon, so I just decided to place their items on the doorsteps. Just then, Lacy came bounding out of her house.

"I love my doll!" Lacy exclaimed when she saw me. "Her name is Cafrine."

I smiled at this, surprised she would name her doll after me, when in all truth, the doll was the exact replica of Maureen.

"Lacy, would you like to help me take these over to Maureen and Mable?" I asked her, holding up some cookies and a huge slice of cherry pie.

"Yes!" Lacy exclaimed, grabbing my hand at once.

When we arrived at the cottage, Mama Mable answered the door.

"Hello," I said, putting on a big smile. "I brought you some desserts from the husking bee."

She grumbled something about leftovers before moving to let me come in.

I stepped across the threshold, looking towards the bed to find Maureen there. Sure enough, there she lay, one heavily foot propped up on a stool, a tattered book on her lap.

"Did you bring something?" Maureen's face brightened, and she squirmed a little, trying to sit up straighter. Mama Mable rushed over and pushed her back down with a gentle shove

"Yes," I said. "It's leftover from last night."

Mama Mable mumbled something else which I didn't hear, but I decided to ignore it.

"Can I have some?" asked Maureen with a hopeful look.

Mama Mable clicked her tongue. "Not 'til after supper, you can't."

A smile played at the corners of my mouth.

Maureen scoffed and eyed me with an aggravated expression. I shot her back a knowing look.

Mama Mable came over and took the dessert from me, placing it on the wooden table. Then she left us, resuming her work in the kitchen. She started out humming something softly, and then her voice did something I never thought it would do. She began to sing. And what came from her mouth wasn't mediocre. It was an exceptional voice, a gorgeous one, low and soulful. It suddenly began escalating to the highest of high notes, then descending to the lowest of the low. I was simply in a daze, listening to her song, which I had never heard before. For a moment, I forgot about everything.

"Pretty voice, ain't it?" Maureen's words startled me.

I nodded. "Yes. A wonderful voice."

I looked at Maureen, who was smiling at me. I smiled back, thankful that she didn't despise me, as I thought she had.

"Well, I better go now," I said, turning to leave, although I would have happily stayed to visit with Maureen and hear Mama Mable sing all afternoon.

"Catherine, you said your name was?" Maureen asked.

I nodded, beaming.

"Was real nice what you did for Lacy. That doll, I mean." She paused, looking down at her lap. "You might come back tomorrow, if you want. We can talk or somethin'. It gets lonely just layin' here."

Did I just hear those blessed words?

"Yes. I would like that," I told her with a golden sincerity. "I would like that very much."

~

The next morning I strolled down by Maureen's house to see how she was doing. When I reached the house, I knocked twice and Mama Mable answered the door. She grunted and opened the door wide enough for me to slip in. I offered her a weak smile only for it to be unnoticed or, rather, ignored. Oh, well.

I found Maureen with her foot propped up in a big, cushioned chair by the fireplace, which was burning with gold and crimson flames. She had her back to me, but I could tell she was reading because I heard her soft murmurs. I was utterly caught off guard. Reading! Most Negroes had no clue as to how to read or write. Actually, slaves were put to death if they were caught with a book. But, I suppose things were different here.

"Hello," I whispered gently, taking a seat in a rocking chair next to her. Maureen glanced up at me and smiled. Then she placed her novel down and looked at me with silver eyes.

"So," I said, unsure of what exactly to say.

"My ankle ain't broken." She gazed into the fire's depths. "Mama Mable says it's only badly strained. I can walk on it in a day or so, whenever I feel up to it."

I nodded. "It's good that it was just a strain."

"But a day is a long time to stay inside."

"It will go by fast." I assured her. "So, you read?"

She stared at me for a moment, and then nodded.

"What book is it?"

"Oh, this is just a hymnal."

How could a person read a book of music? "Oh."

"I love to sing. I wanna be as good as Mama Mable someday. But I ain't good at any instruments and I think if I could really hear the way the music sounds I could be a real good singer."

Joy overflowed in my heart. "I have a piano! I could accompany you!"

Maureen's eyes lit up like stars, but then muddled with confusion. "Accompany?"

111

"I mean, I could play for you so you could hear the way the notes are supposed to sound."

She beamed. "That would be lovely!"

I nodded. We sat silent for a moment.

"How'd you learn to play the piano?" she asked timidly.

I proceeded to tell Maureen all about the piano lessons. And she was so interested in my story that I began telling her all about my school lessons, which soon led to all about my childhood. I didn't know it, but in a few minutes, I had told Maureen each and every thing about my past, including the love I had felt deprived of as a little girl and why I was in Saint Louis, anyway. By the end of the story, both of us were in tears. Mama Mable must have listened in, also, for there were tears streaming down her crinkled, brown face. And right then, I believe Maureen and I became friends.

~

"Gloomy weather" greeted us that afternoon, just as Andrew had read from the morning paper. But I didn't think of it as gloomy at all. The rain was calming to me, the thunder entrancing; I was inspired to draw. Collecting my notebook and sharpened pencil, I stepped out into the misty, gray air, all at once blown away by the power of the rainstorm. The water came down in blankets, and I had to sit far underneath the verandah so I wouldn't get my precious paper wet. I decided to draw a landscape, a picture of the barn and the everlasting fields. Cows were grazing, and I intended to include them in my picture, also. Once again, I felt the need to capture that moment onto paper to have and keep always. I wished I could include all the sounds I heard, the soft thumping of the rain as it hit the welcoming, thirsty ground, the clashing of thunder and the low moos of the cows. I wanted anyone who looked at my drawings to feel the same way I felt at that moment, but drawings were just drawings. I really couldn't make someone look at my picture and feel the same way as I did.

After my rough sketch was finished, I worked on shading each object to perfection, the shadows of the barn and the spots on the cows. And just when I signed my signature on the bottom, the screen door creaked and I had no time to shove and hide away my picture. It was too late. Jonathon was at my side, asking me to please show him what I had.

"I don't have anything," I assured him, covering my picture as well as I could with my hands. "Honestly."

"Aw, come on, Catherine. Please show me?"

He sounded like an eager school boy, and I laughed shortly, nervous-like.

"No. Now don't you have work to do?" I asked swiftly, eager to get him away.

He sat down beside me on the porch swing, and my nerves escalated. "Not in this rain. My mother just wanted to know why you're out here. Should I'll tell her you're drawing obscene pictures and wish to be left alone?"

I gasped, but he only laughed. "You wouldn't dare!"

"No, I wouldn't. But, please. Just show me," he pleaded, blue eyes open and innocent.

"Why should I?" I knew I was being impossible, and I didn't care.

He stared at me for a moment, leaning coolly back into the seat, face smug and eyes blue and curious. I felt my cheeks burn. Why did he stare at me so?

"Please?" The word was spoken so soft and so sweet that something inside me just bent. And so I took a deep breath and handed over the sketchbook.

"I'm not all the way finished, but—" I stopped when his face transformed. He glanced up at me, the smile gone.

"How did you learn to draw like this? This is amazing!" He flipped through the whole journal, observing each and every piece. I wanted to object, but something in his eyes made me stop.

"Who is this?" His blue eyes were quizzical as he turned to the portrait of Milly.

"My old chambermaid."

"Your slave?"

"She was more like a mother to me than anything." My eyes lingered on the horizon as if any minute Milly might appear. "I loved her more than anyone."

"What about your mother and father? Didn't you love them?" he asked, eyes deep with concern.

"I'm not sure," I looked down at my lap, ashamed. "Milly loved me more than they ever did, though."

He combed through some more pages, ending up on the sketch I'd drawn of Belle.

"Our horse?" he asked.

"Yes. Belle—" I stopped myself.

"What?"

"What is her name?" I hurried to ask.

"Well, she doesn't really have an official name yet. You're welcome to name her. If you want to."

My lips curled at the ends. "Belle?"

He smiled. Handing back my sketchbook, Jonathon became deadly quiet. He seemed focused, content with the silence.

"Would you like to ride her?"

I glimmered in veneration. "Yes, please."

"Really?" He sat up straighter, a huge smile lining his face.

I nodded. A silent moment passed, and I watched his face, memorizing every line, every detail, every curve.

"Maybe when it stops raining?" I offered.

~

My cup of excitement was well over its brim when the storm finally decided to cease. The sun was hanging heavy in the sky, and at any minute I wouldn't have been surprised if it had fell right down into the clouds. After an unusually early dinner, I descended out into the evening to do my last chores, half-hoping Jonathon would follow me. Actually, he'd been rather quiet during dinner, and he hadn't even looked at me.

The barn was dark as I stepped inside, and immediately my breath was knocked out of my lungs as a sudden force pulled me by the waist. I let out a startled scream as I realized the force was a man's hands.

Jonathon's recognizable laughter filled my ears, and I breathed out in relief.

"You're awful." I scolded, but a secret smile tugged at my lips.

I noticed the way his hands lingered on my waist another moment as he said, "Still up for a ride?"

I blinked in the darkness. "Yes."

And with that simple word, Jonathon grasped my hand and whisked me away to the horses' outdoor stables. I felt my cheeks burn red at his hand covering mine, conscious of the smallness of mine under his. He led me through the stables, and as we passed by all the long, sober faces of the horses, I fell in love instantly with each one. How beautiful and unique they were! We stopped in front of Belle, and Jonathon unlocked the gates, whispering to her. She came thumping out, each step slow and precise. I immediately felt tiny, like the horse was a giant and I was a mere blade of grass. The worry must have shown on my face, for Jonathon pulled me gently forward by my hand.

"She won't hurt you," he assured me. "I promise."

And then he fastened a saddle onto her hide, fingers working with skill and ease.

"Well?" he said, and I stared at him.

"You want me to climb up?" I asked.

And then he joked sarcastically, "Ladies first." I caught the amused twinkle of mockery in his dancing blue eyes.

"No. Not this time." And I meant it.

"Suit yourself," he said as he pulled himself up onto the saddle with great ease.

I grasped his outstretched hand firmly as he pulled me up behind him.

How tall I felt! And how frightening it was! I held onto Jonathon's hand, and when he tried to free it, I squeezed harder. I couldn't help it; I was scared! He laughed and instructed me to wrap my hands around his waist if I was afraid. At first I hesitated, thinking it a terribly improper thing to do, but I did it anyway, my body pressed tightly against his. We were so close that I could hardly draw a breath without him knowing. My heart nearly jumped out of my skin as the horse started to move forward, and when we came to the open barn gates, she broke into a trot. I didn't know where Jonathon planned on taking me, and I didn't dare ask. I was frightened to even breathe, much less ask him a question. Belle seemed to know where she was going; in a minute we were headed across the miles of grassy hills and fields. I found myself relaxing against Jonathon's warm and welcoming body, and I could actually feel the rhythmic movement of his muscles and his heartbeat.

My eyes traveled the length of the horizon, streaked vibrant reds and soft pinks. The wind whipped back my hair, making my whole body prickle with gooseflesh. I inhaled the fresh fragrance of the outdoors, wondering what other kinds of places were as perfect as this. And then I thought of Jonathon, which caused my breathing to come in short rasps and make my head spin and my blood curdle. I wondered if he could feel my heartbeat, too. I wondered what he was thinking. Even though I tried not to think of the intensity of his blues eyes, to think about the sunset or something else, instead, I couldn't. Not even for a moment. Jonathon cleared his throat, and I started.

"All right?" he laughed, sending a glance back to me. I blushed, and I glad he couldn't see me.

"Where are we going?" It seemed like I had to scream for him to hear me.

He shook his head, and I caught a sly part of smile on his mouth. "You'll see. There are two places I want to show you."

I pursed my lips and exhaled deeply. Thankfully, I was able to relax and allow my mind to drift away. How amazing the night was! And from this view, it was even better. Such blazing color! It was a wonder how beautiful Nature could be. Try as I might, never would I beat Mother Nature in an art contest. For She was the one who paints the skies, the one who sweeps the Earth with rain and dots the green grass with vivid flowers. No, I would never compare to her as an artist.

I fell so deep into my thoughts that I began to doze off. A moment later I awoke with a jolt, my eyes fluttering open as I observed my surroundings. The sky was tinted a shade darker, the air calmer and softer. The sun no longer lingered above the horizon, and only a mere glow of what was left brightened the blue-violet sky. Only then did I realize that we had stopped, right in the middle of a huge prairie which I didn't recognize at all. Nothing surrounded me except grass and flourishing trees that bordered far away, and an old, red barn that stood in a tumble of weeds. But it was neither the barn nor the prairie that caught my attention. It was a small, wooden sign that hung on a pole close to the rickety fence. And in carved letters were the words, "Free Spirits." They were carved precisely and accurately, and I wondered who could have been capable of such craftsmanship. Before my mouth could utter a single inquiry, Jonathon stooped down from the horse, eyes looking up at me expectantly. He brought up his hand, and I took it warily, trying my best to get off the horse without making a fool of myself. Better said than done. When I released my first foot from the stirrup, I practically tripped my way down, falling right into Jonathon. He caught me with both arms, steadying me.

"You all right?" he asked, trying hard not to laugh.

I nodded, pushing myself upright and brushing off the imaginary dust from my skirts.

"What is this place?" I asked, eyes traveling the length of the horizon laid out before me. I took a better look at the old barn, the rickety fence, and the endless miles of lush grass. But when I caught a glance of the exquisite sign, my gaze was captured and held. What a mysterious place.

"This," Jonathon spread out his arms, a playful smile tugging on his lips. "is Free Spirits, a magical place that people travel the world just to see."

I stared at him as if his mind had blown away with the sudden gust of wind.

"Whatever are you talking about?" I could feel giggles rise up in my throat.

Jonathon laughed, strolling over to a stump. I looked about me, and seeing nowhere for me to sit, I just spread out my skirts and settled myself right down on a strip of dewed grass. I could tell he was deep in thought by the way his eyebrows made a creasing line down the center of his forehead. I noticed that line before, once at the dinner table. Suddenly he glanced up at me, as if noting my presence for the first time.

"Anna Mae and I, we made this place. At first, we were just exploring the property one afternoon, and we stumbled upon this big, empty grassland. The only things that were here was this barn and that fence over there. We crept inside that barn and found all sorts of things. We didn't know what it was, or why it was still there, and we never even told our parents. They still don't know. And so I got a piece of wood and Anna Mae got a hammer, and we went to work on that sign." He chuckled, looking into the distance. "It took me four days to get those words perfect.

"And so this was our land. We pretended we were two western settlers on the wide, open prairie, all alone in the vast wilderness. Every chance we got, we hurried down here to play. We ran like wild Indians in the grass, played cowboys and cowgirls with pretend horses, and just had the time of our lives here. And it truly was a land for free spirits, you know. 'Cause we were. I can remember the memories we had here. It's unbearable to think that she's gone. Gone forever. It's not fair at all. And to think I could have saved her . . ."

I took his hand on a sudden impulse, and as I stared into his blue eyes, I saw them suddenly start to melt, like ice finding a hot stream of sunshine. And then once again, his eyes were warm and gentle, the way they were supposed to be, the way I liked them. Then the spell ended and I took my hand away, my fingers threading together in my lap, my throat dry and scratchy.

"You know," I said, eyes near to tears. "You can't keep doing this to yourself. God obviously called her to Heaven that day for a reason. It was out of your hands." I couldn't believe the words had escaped from my own lips. I was talking about God with Jonathon?

He studied me with deep intensity. And then suddenly, a crack of thunder interrupted what he was about to say.

A second later, dark, hovering clouds clashed together, causing huge drops of rain to fall everywhere. We darted up, running for cover. I followed Jonathon into the little barn, and by the time we got there, our bodies were soaked to the bone. I kicked off my muddy boots and wrung out my wet petticoats, scoffing. Only earlier that day I had adored the rain, but now it had deceived me.

Jonathon stripped off his boots, too, taking a seat on a little stool fit for a child, much less a nineteen-year old boy. His face was turned down in a deep, infuriated smug. The whole thing was ridiculous, and I tried to stifle a giggle, but it was too late. My voice evaporated into a million laughs, and I couldn't help them. Jonathon stared at me for a moment with eyes of steel. I might have just been told a hilarious joke, not just received a cold drenching of rain. But a moment later, he was laughing, too, and when the laughter finally died out, we sat in utter silence, each buried in our own worlds of bottomless thought.

After a moment, Jonathon moved to the empty door of the barn, staring out into the dark, rainy evening. Before I knew what I was doing, I was there, too, gazing. Jonathon turned to me, eyes unreadable, but still warm and full of admiration. For me. Not for the barn, or for Anna Mae, or for Free Spirits. For me. I was sure of it.

In a second too soon, the spell ended, and the rain came to a halt. It was getting dark; the first shade of darkness had already claimed its place in the sky. Jonathon announced we should leave, and as I moved over to where Belle stood grazing, I tried as best as I could to dodge each and every mud puddle. But my clumsiness gave away, and I tripped on a sharp rock only to get my boot caught firmly in a nice-sized puddle of gooey, brown mud. I groaned aloud.

"What?" Jonathon whirled around and then recoiled at the sight of my boots sinking deeper. I held up my skirts high as he tried to free my foot. Oh, wouldn't have Miss Mortemeyer just died! In addition to the mud, which ladies were never supposed to involve themselves with, gentlemen simply did not touch a proper young lady's ankle, or any other body part for that matter. But Jonathon was *not* a gentleman, and I was not a proper young lady—anymore at least. In a second, my foot was free, but my poor boot was not. I stood on one foot for a moment, until Jonathon caught me up in his arms. Once he brought me over to the horse, he cautiously set me up onto the saddle, and without a word, he trailed back over to retrieve my silly boot. The smile that lined his face made me want to roll up in a ball and die of mortification.

That night in bed, I relived the whole evening. And then I wondered at what Jonathon had said.

"There are two places . . ."

What of the second?

My mind soon trailed off to Maureen and how she seemed so attentive about what I'd had to say. It truly seemed like she'd wanted to know more about me, wanted to talk to me. And maybe in time she would care to tell me about her past.

Just as I was on the verge of drifting to sleep, I heard another sound, the clashing magnificence of thunder. Rain yet again? My senses fully awoke, and I listened very carefully. Finally, the well-expected rain darted to the earth, pelting the ground. But then, straining my ears to hear beyond the storm, I heard the distinct sound of scampering feet. A commotion downstairs and the banging on the door made my sharpened senses freeze. More fugitives?

Tip-toeing out of my room and down the hallway, I paused at the top of the staircase. I saw many shadows in dim, flickering candlelight. They silently whispered to one another, and I had to listen carefully to catch what was exchanged.

"She's hurt," a woman cried softly.

"Yes, very badly. I'll need to get my wife, Anna."

Andrew's footsteps hurried toward the stairs, but I called out to him.

"Andrew, I'll wake Anna," I told him confidently, with more assurance than I really had.

"Oh . . . Catherine! Thank you, dear. Tell her to come quick," he whispered up the staircase.

I rushed into their bedroom, pausing when I saw her figure cuddled under the deep quilts.

"Anna," I whispered.

Immediately her eyes shot open in alarm. "What is it?"

"Fugitives," I answered, suddenly unsure of what to say. "Andrew needs your help. Someone is hurt."

In a split second, Anna was up and running past me, mumbling under her breath. I scrambled after her, bumping into Jonathon on my way out. Startled, I landed on my bottom with a thud.

"Good heavens . . ." I muttered, smoothing my nightdress.

Without a word, Jonathon pulled me to my feet and gently brushed a stray curl away from my face.

"Come on," he said quietly. "Go back to bed. Mama likes to handle these things herself."

I stared at him with blank eyes. "But . . . what if she needs my—"

"Don't worry. I learned this lesson before. Once she's on the case, no help will be accepted. Now go back to bed."

"Please let me help," I begged, "Let me at least offer to help. I want to."

Jonathon sighed and allowed me to pass him, and I descended the staircase with quick legs.

~

The woman's face remained completely and utterly still as Anna applied the poultice to her forehead. She had been unconscious by the time the fugitives came, and even now her grim expression hinted at death, I daresay. Apparently the woman had fallen, hitting her head. It was hard for me to sit and watch as Anna gently dressed the wound. The poor woman let a small groan evaporate from her barely open lips, and her eyes rolled upward. A large man from the group had taken Emmy up in his arms, placing her in one of the other guest beds Anna had offered.

"Tsk. Tsk. It's all right, dear," Anna coaxed. "Just be still. We saw to your friends and made sure they were comfortable in the cellar. They all agree that it might be best for you to spend the night here and rest yourself, as you've taken quite a fall. They're all settled and rested now. Just rest yourself, now."

The woman's eyes flickered open, revealing a beautiful pair of gray eyes. Just like Maureen's. They shut slowly again.

"And by the way, my name is Anna Walter."

A weak smile formed on the woman's lips, and she opened her mouth to speak. "I'm Emmy Jacobs."

"Now you'll just rest here for the night, Emmy."

~

That next day, the sun shone brightly through the silver clouds, although the general mood created by the new fugitives was quite nerve-racking. The Walters were upset about the incident of the night before, and I'm sure the slaves were, too. The poor woman rested on the bed, curtains draped shut so the darkness would provide a safe, comforting atmosphere for her. The others waited patiently in the downstairs cellar, resting and preparing themselves for what was to come. A plan was not in its final molds, but the overall idea was that the fugitives would leave that night. Andrew and Jonathon would lead them to the river and help them get across. However, if Emmy did not feel well enough to make the mile-long journey, the plan would not be carried through.

Looking in on Emmy, I shook my head. The woman was still obviously in pain, for she slept all day. It appeared as though she would never wake up.

To distract her from her worrying, Anna had asked that I play something nice for her on the piano. She rummaged through the piano bench to find all sorts of music for me. Immediately I lost myself in the sheet music, eyes scanning the titles. *Amazing Grace*, a song I knew well, caught my eye instantly. I set it before me on the piano, composing myself.

The soft autumn breeze glided through the open windows, pulling my tangling curls away from my face. I closed my eyes momentarily as I played the chorus of the beloved song. Sweet, golden sunshine played upon the keys. Goosebumps tingled up and down my arms as I played, and my heart began to quicken its pace. I don't know why such things happened when I played the piano, but they just did. Anna listened carefully for a time, and then told me she would be back in a minute, as she had to discuss something with Andrew.

I played on despite her absence, but moments after her departure, a sudden knock on the door startled me, and I jumped back from the piano. Sweeping my skirts off the floor, I glided over to the door and peeked out the open window. A young man dressed sharply in a blue uniform stood on the porch. He carried a bundle with him, and in his hand was a telegram.

Tucking a loose curl behind my ear, I pulled on the doorknob.

"Ah, hello," the blond man smiled. "I have a telegram for a Mr. Andrew Walter."

"Oh, of course," I returned, taking the telegram. "Thank you very much, sir."

Once the mail carrier was out of sight, I yanked up my skirts and flew outside, set on delivering the telegram personally. Finding the Walters out back, I slowed down my pace.

"Andrew!" I called urgently. "I have a telegram!"

He smiled and held out his hand, and I placed the mail into it. But when he started reading it, his eyes grew fearful. Running a hand through his hair, he called Anna over.

"What is it, darlin'?" she asked with a touch of worry in her voice.

"Just read this."

When Anna placed a hand on her heart, I knew something was wrong. Curiosity burned inside me; I wanted to know what the telegram said. But my manners told me to remain silent, so I reluctantly pursed my lips.

"Oh, praise be! Look at poor Catherine. She's just as worried as us!" Anna smiled sweetly, placing her hand on my shoulder. "Go ahead, Andrew. Tell her what has happened."

"Well, it's a notice for us. It says that there's slave catcher going to be around the neighborhood. It says he will be here by tomorrow morning. The slaves must leave tonight, in that case. How is the woman?"

"Still resting," Anna sighed. "I should go check on her again within the hour. Well, we best not be worryin' bout it now. There's work to be done. Catherine, that piano piece was beautiful. Please keep playin' it. It's a joy to listen to."

Never mind the piano. I wanted to ask Anna questions. There wasn't anything I hated more than having questions unanswered. Absolutely nothing more. Shuffling back into the house, I stopped when I saw Maureen coming across the open, empty fields. She limped slightly, but she came quickly, all the same. Her foot was still wrapped up tightly, but despite that, her image was a perfect one. A radiant smile bowed her pretty face, and she waved when she saw me.

"Hello," she greeted me. "You wanna play for me today?"

I was glad for the distraction, but even gladder that Maureen had come to see me.

Once inside, I led her over to the piano bench, where we settled down together.

"Was this song in your hymnal?" I asked, pointing to the sheet music. "*Amazing Grace?*"

Her eyes lit up. "Oh, yes."

"Good. Shall we?" I asked, glancing at her with a smile.

"Yes. Go ahead."

My fingers hit the keys, and Maureen cleared her throat, staring intently at the sheet music. She began to sing at once. I was so blown away by the first verse evaporating off of Maureen's lips that I almost forgot to move my fingers on the piano. Her voice was so unique . . . It was not a rough perfection like Mama Mable's, it was a sheer smooth trickle of gold. Her voice rose to the high notes, conquered the low ones, and made the song into something more than just a hymn. She made it her own, with soul and ingenuity. I was absolutely speechless. Her perfect voice sent tiny spirals racing up my spine. My flesh prickled, and all I could do was keep playing her the notes on the piano.

After the song, I stood in complete surprise, chills rushing down my back.

"You . . . you're amazing. Maureen, how did you ever learn how to sing so?"

She blushed. "I just . . . I don't know. Catherine?"

"Yes?" I answered, eyes widening.

"You know, I really felt like . . . like we have come to know each other better." She was studying her fingers, and I knew she was having trouble on choosing her words. I didn't blame her.

"I felt that same way." I gave her a sweet smile, and she met my eyes and smiled back.

"And I ain't never had a friend my age, you know. I know this probably ain't how you go about this, but do you think you'd like me as a friend?"

My smile broadened.

"More than anything."

Her whole face brightened and glowed. "You know how you told me 'bout that fire at your house and your mother and father? Well, your story kind of reminds me of mine. You wanna hear it?"

I couldn't believe it! She actually trusted me enough to share her life story with me. I was genuinely touched.

Nodding solemnly, I said, "And I'll listen to each and every word. Just like you did for me."

She smiled and looked towards the ceiling, gathering her thoughts. "It all started out when I was nine years old. My mama and I was slaves down in Arkansas. And all my life, I'd worked hard in the fields and done all sorts of stuff for my massa. I had a sister, too. I loved her like crazy. She was younger than me, only five at the time. I was about eleven, I guess. Every day I'd hear the other slaves talk about freedom, and I wondered if it was true. If there really was a place where Negroes could be free. And then one day my mama decided to take me and my sister away. They were plannin' on going to the place where they could be free. And so we ran away at night, when the North Star was shinin' in the black sky, and we followed it north until the sun came up. I can remember the night like yesterday. So dark . . . and as cold as ice. We ran for days, it seemed. Then we would hide in the woods when the sun was out, not makin' a peep all day. It was scary, 'cause my mama would be cryin' real quiet like. And my sister and I didn't know what was goin' on, and so we just stayed real quiet. And then we went to this house. A family with white folks put us in a little, secret room and gave us food and water. And it was dark and scary in there, too, and my mama kept whisperin' things to me. Things that broke my heart, that I still remember. She said, 'You know I love you. You know that whatever happens, I love you and always will.'

"And then one day, a white man with evil, golden eyes broke into the secret room. I swear his eyes were gold. I can still see them."

Maureen stared into the distance, face somber and cool. A single tear rolled down her cheek.

"And he and some other white men shoved us into a wagon with a lot of other Negroes and chained our feet and hands so we couldn't move. And then when the golden-eyed man wasn't payin' attention, my mama told me to get out of the wagon and run with my sister. She told me to slip the chains off my hands and feet since I was small, and do the same for my sister. And I did. I grabbed up my little sister in my arms, even though I wasn't much bigger than her myself, and I jumped off the wagon and ran. The white man didn't see me, and so I just kept runnin' even though I didn't know where I was goin'. And I only looked back once to see my poor mama, tears runnin' down her pretty face.

"Well we spent that night in the woods, and my sister fell awfully ill. And we was so tired and hungry, and we traveled on for another day, not really knowing where to go or what to do. We was searching for help, someone or something to guide us. That night we saw a light coming from a house in the distance. I carried my sister up to the house and knocked on the door, hoping whoever was in the house would help us. Now that I think about it, I don't know why I was so trusting. I should've been afraid, but I was so desperate, I figured anyone would have pity on us. A woman answered the door. That woman was Anna Walter. She led me inside; I remember thinking I was in heaven. And then she gave us food and coffee, and I told her how we got there. And that night she gave us a room to sleep in and tended to my sister, although death was lurking in the shadows of her little face, and we all knew it. The next morning, my little sister was gone. She was stone still and cold as ice underneath those warm blankets Anna had given her.

"Well, after that happened, everythin' went by in a blur. Anna let me stay there, and she introduced me to the servants, and I soon began helpin' around the house. I lived in one of the cabins with Mama Mable, who became like a mother to me, and I was grateful.

"Over the years I have thought to myself. I have wondered if my mama is still alive. And sometimes I'd think so hard on that that I would have these terrible headaches and just feel like dyin' myself. I know this sounds bad, but I've wished I was dead probably a hundred times. It's not that I don't like the Walters or Mama Mable or anybody. It's just that I miss my *real* family. I want my mama back. I miss my baby sister. But I know I'll never see any of them again. And it just hurts so bad. I can't even explain how bad it hurts, to know you just have to keep livin', to know life just keeps goin'. I feel like life just is draggin' me by a weak thread."

"Maureen," I whispered with a cracked voice. "Have you ever . . . talked to God? Have you ever prayed to Him?"

Maureen stared at me a moment with puzzled eyes before replying, "I don't know how to pray."

I took both of her hands in mine, holding them tight. "I feel that way, sometimes."

"I don't understand. If He is real, then why's so much pain in the world? Why do white folks get all they want, and us Negroes suffer each day?"

I sat silent awhile, concentrating on what she'd said.

"I'm not sure I can answer that. There is a lot of evil in the world, Maureen, and God wants us to try and overcome it. He wants us to pray to Him, and put our faith in Him. And if we do, I think we'll have a better chance of overcoming all that evil." The words came tumbling out of my mouth. I don't know where they came from, but they empowered me.

Maureen's glassy eyes changed from despair to realization. She nodded, closing her eyes for a moment.

"What if He doesn't answer my prayers?"

I bit my lip, and answered confidently, "Do you have anything to lose?"

She shook her head, eyes still closed. I closed mine as well, holding her hands in mine. "Would you start for me?"

I sighed. "God, if You're there, would you please listen to what Maureen has to say?"

I paused to let Maureen finish.

"God, I never did pray before. Mama Mable wanted me to, but I didn't. And so I'm askin' forgiveness for that. I need You. I need help. And I'm sorry if this is a lousy prayer, but I ain't much good at it. Please, I'm askin' for a sign. Please show me that you're listenin' to me. Anyway, Amen."

By the time she finished, we were both in tears. We had both been moved by an incredible, inaudible, invisible force.

"Excuse me." Emmy Jacobs stood on the stairwell, peering down at us.

The woman flashed her sparkling gray eyes toward me, then to Maureen. Her gaze locked, and her jaw fell. I glanced over to Maureen and found that her face was one of utter shock. Standing up slowly, she glided across the room, face retaining its astonished expression.

"Maureen?" the woman asked in a terribly low whisper.

"Mama." Maureen spoke as if the whole world had changed.

In the next minute, they clung to each other desperately, exchanging tears and hugs and kisses. Mother and daughter smiled graciously in sweet reunion, and I stared in complete amazement. Tears of joy streamed from their eyes like waterfalls, and squeals of happiness evaporated from their lips. I couldn't believe my eyes.

That was a sign if I'd ever seen one.

I slipped out the back door silently, leaving the two alone. God's overwhelming power had brought Maureen to her mother. And all Maureen had to do was ask for it. The irony and power of it all made me want to dance around the house and sing to the heavens. And I almost would have, too, if Jonathon wouldn't have shot around the house at that exact minute. I raced to Him, telling him of the good news. For a moment he stared blankly at me, letting the words sink in.

"For goodness sake, did you tell my parents?"

"No, not yet. Where are they?"

"They just went inside, I think."

I gasped. Without another word, I grabbed Jonathon's hand, and together, we hurried into the house, arriving breathless. Anna and Andrew were talking to Maureen and her mother. I noticed immediately how much they resembled each other.

". . . all I did was pray," Maureen was saying. When she spotted me, her face glowed and she rushed toward me. "Why didn't you tell me God answers prayers so fast?"

"Well, I . . ." I began to respond, but Anna took over. "I didn't know."

Emmy smiled at her daughter, placing a kiss on her forehead. "I can't believe it. I just been prayin' all my life for this. God sure does answer prayers. He sure does."

"I'm sorry to have to bring this up, but we must talk about it now. I'm afraid there will be no other time to do so," Andrew apologized, his tone expressing his sudden worry. "You see, Time is of the essence, and I'm afraid we won't be able to wait another night to make the escape. There is a slave catcher in town tomorrow, and I want you all to be gone by the time he comes."

Emmy nodded, looking into her daughter's eyes. The question was evident—Would Maureen join her mother and the others on the journey north, or would they both stay at the Walters' home?

~

Later on that day, as Maureen and her mother walked the open fields, conversing endlessly, I paced nervously in my room. Maureen wouldn't leave the Walters' farm, would she? Surely her mother would want to stay here too, with her daughter. The Walters would be more than happy to oblige, wouldn't they? My thoughts were disturbed because of a soft rapping at the door.

"Come in," I called.

Jonathon opened the door. "Can I borrow you for a moment, Miss Carey?"

I smiled and took his hand, a bubbling excitement surging through me, distracting me from my fretting.

He led me outside through the back door. Anna stared quizzically after us, and I pinched up my face to show her I knew nothing of her son's odd behavior. The evening was coming upon us; the brown leaves crumpled underneath our feet with every step. Jonathon told me to close my eyes, and I obeyed, a little hesitantly at first. It was suddenly chilly, and I wished dearly for my muslin shawl. I didn't know where he was taking me, or why, but—the second place! Of course! When I was allowed to open my eyes, I found that we stood in front of a gigantic weeping willow tree. I'd never seen it before. Glancing around, I saw the house not so far away. It had been in the backyard all this time, and I'd never known? It was beautiful and majestic; I marveled at it.

"Come on." Jonathon led me through the branches, pushing back the drooping leaves thoughtfully. "I want to show you this."

We stopped once we reached the wide trunk of the tree. I could only imagine how old the pioneer willow was. The view from the inside was even more amazing! I felt like a tiny child again, playing princess with a willow tree for my castle. I was very conscious of the way Jonathon's body radiated warmth, the way he smiled at me in the twilight. I looked to where he was pointing, on the base of the tree's trunk, and I could barely make out a phrase of words carved neatly, just like the sign of Free Spirits. Except these words were smaller and more delicate.

"This tree is dedicated to . . ." I couldn't make out the next words. Jonathon took out a match out of his pocket and struck it, lighting up the last words so that I could see. My name.

"Catherine Carey." Jonathon spoke my name, and I shivered at the sound of it, staring at him. He dismissed my startled gaze and read on, voice soft and gentle and low. "A free spirit."

"Why did you do this for me?" I fingered every detail of the carved dedication.

But the night was so soft and Jonathon was so close, I forgot the whole world. Before I could utter a single word, his lips were pressed softly onto mine, and in that moment, my wish came true. He released me, and I gazed up into eyes bluer than I'd remembered. The kiss had been brief. It was like a tiny sip of lemonade, delicious and giving me mixed sensations, and I craved more. As if Jonathon thought the exact same thing, he brought his head down again, and

I inhaled his uniquely wonderful scent once more before he captivated me in a long, capacious kiss that was even better than the first. It was as if a wild prairie had been lighted with a single flame, for the kiss expanded and flourished, and I couldn't help but melt in his arms. I wrapped my arms around him, pulling him closer, and he enveloped me in his arms solidly, yet gently, as if I was a delicate rose not to be too firmly handled with. It soon ended, breathlessly, and Jonathon led me back through the leaves, up the hill, and back into the house.

~

Maureen met me when I entered the living room, seated on the piano bench.

"What are you doing here?" I asked, smiling.

"I wanted to talk to you about tonight." Her eyes were grave and filled with unshed tears.

And before she even began to speak, I knew. I didn't want to hear it. I knew she was going to say goodbye to me, that she was going to leave me and the Walters, and I couldn't bear it.

"Why must you go?" I asked, taking her hands in mine. "Stay here! Tell your mother to stay with us, too!"

"Catherine . . ." Maureen drifted off, looking all over the room, avoiding my eyes. "I'm sorry. I'm goin' where my mama goes. She thinks there's something better for us, and I have to trust her."

"But it's so dangerous!" I exclaimed.

"I know," Maureen sighed.

At that moment, I lost it. I fell beside her on the piano bench and cried. We had known each other for such a short time, and yet I felt like she was my sister. How could she abandon me? How could she leave everything she knew and all the people that loved her? Where did her mother think she was going, anyway?

"Do you want to play for me one more time?" Maureen asked, wiping away her tears.

I held her gaze for a moment before allowing my eyes to rest upon the beloved instrument. My fingers traced swiftly this time, violently. Maureen placed a hand on my shoulder and started in with the lyrics to "Amazing Grace". I marveled at the magic of music that we made together. Her voice rose and fell in perfection, and my fingers tapped out the song to complement her singing, and for a moment, I was lost in the song.

When it was over, Maureen turned to me.

"I have something to say," Maureen announced with sparkling eyes. "I prayed to God about this. He answered me, 'cause I know what I have to do. You brought me to God, who brought me to my mama. And I know that if I follow her, I will be able do somethin' else with my life. I'll be able help more of my people escape to freedom, and I will be able to be free. I'll be able to help people find God, the same way you helped me. And that's exactly what I'm gonna do."

Tears uncontrollably welled up in my eyes, and my throat burned with upset.

"I want you to come down and say goodbye to me at the river," she said with hopeful eyes.

~

That night, I waited quietly in my room. Jonathon said he would send for me when it was time. I watched the hands of the clock with impatient eyes.

Soon, I found myself drifting deep into my own thoughts. How I had changed since I came to Missouri.

The old Catherine Carey was gone. The girl who was in her place was so different . . . She was more sure of herself. She actually had a purpose in her life. She had things to look forward to. She had people to love. But sadly, one thing remained the same. She still had to say her goodbyes.

How had Maureen inhabited such a dear place in my heart, anyway? I hadn't known her long at all. And yet, something about her drew me to her. Nevermind the fact that our skin colors weren't the same. Perhaps Jonathon had been right after all. Perhaps Pastor Dominic had been speaking about equality all along. And perhaps the Walters weren't wrong in helping slaves to freedom. Despite how I had been raised, and how I had been expected to feel about Negroes my whole life up until now, a sudden realization began to dawn on me. Many of the most sincere, truly good people I've come to know in my life are Negroes. Didn't that mean something?

And for the first time in a long time, I kneeled to the ground before my bed. I folded my hands and sat for a minute in silence, absorbed in my thoughts. Suddenly, words floated out of my mouth.

"God. I don't know what I'm doing right now. It's been so long since I've tried to talk to You. I feel like my life, up until now, has been so closed-off. I've been inside this tight little bubble, almost. I've been taught how to make proper conversation at a dinner table, and I have been taught how to properly conduct myself in society. But what I wasn't taught growing up . . . What I never learned in that dreadful school, was how to love people. And I think . . . I think that's what Milly tried to show me. That's what Cook and Gordon and everyone wanted to show me. And they did. But now everything seems so clear. I feel like my whole life I was so sheltered, so conformed to think and believe what society wanted me to believe. Here, it's different. I like it here. I'm free here. So, I suppose what I want to say right now is thank You. Thank You for the Walters. Thank you for Nina and Nathaniel and little Lacy. Thank you for Mallory. And thank you for Maureen. And thank you for freedom—"

I started when a soft knock came at my door, but I was up in a second, grabbing my shawl quickly before meeting Andrew and Jonathon.

We went around to the cellar and helped the slaves up. Maureen grasped my hand, and I smiled at her with hopeful eyes. The Walter men led us into the night, and we ran silently, moving swiftly. A mile lay long in front of us, and I became utterly determined to keep up with Jonathon. We came to a small creek smothered with sharp rocks and a freezing flow of stream. I tried dodging the coarse pebbles, but I accidentally tripped over one, nearly falling to my doom. Jonathon caught and steadied me, his smile encouraging me to press onward.

It was the longest ten minutes of my life, panting and breathless and eager to get to the river. But my heart was set, and I didn't give up. My persistence never gave out, and when I thought I was going to faint, I caught a glimpse of a glimmering body of water right over the hill. Even though I felt like screaming for joy, I remained silent as my eyes rested upon the sight in front of me. A wooden boat sailed toward us across the Mississippi, a dark figure clad in long, black robes controlling the paddles. The fugitives stood on the bank, earnestly awaiting the figure's arrival.

When Maureen spotted me, she rushed to me, feet silently thumping across the wet, grassy ground. I reluctantly let go of Jonathon's hand to meet Maureen half way. Tears streamed down my face like waterfalls as I impulsively threw my arms around Maureen for the last time.

"I will always remember, you, Catherine. Always and forever."

"Oh, I will always remember you, dear Maureen. Write to me, will you?"

Maureen pulled back to look into my face. Her silver eyes overflowed with tears.

"Yes, I will. Oh, Catherine, thank you so much. If not for you, I wouldn't have found my mother. I wouldn't have been brave enough to do this. I wouldn't be inspired like I am now. You brought me to God. You brought me back to life. And I will always be thankful for you."

I trembled as Maureen pulled away, moving toward her mother. The boat was here, and the dark figure stood in the boat, making room for the fugitives boarding.

I watched as Maureen departed, expecting to feel a hole of loss burning inside of me. Instead, I felt renewed and empowered, strengthened by the loss. It was a feeling I know would last, a feeling that God had bestowed upon me. Eyes fixed on the departing boat, I blinked the tears away and rubbed my shivering arms. They were free now. They were all free. And then, Jonathon moved behind me, wrapping his breathtakingly warm, comforting arms around me. Pulling me closer, he kissed my cheek tenderly.

"They're going to be free, Catherine. Just like you and me."

December 1854

St. Louis, Missouri

How can I tell you of my ecstasy? There is just so much to tell. Jonathon and I are to be married in May, when I turn eighteen. Anna and Andrew are still avid conductors of the Underground Railroad, and Jonathon and I plan to continue the "family tradition" once we are comfortably suited on a large portion of the Walter's generously-sized farm.

Milly found out my new address in St. Louis, and writes to me frequently. She and her husband, Jack, are happily living in Ontario and plan to visit me one of these days.

And now I must tell you about dear Maureen. She and her mother are living in Winnipeg, enjoying the excitement and freedoms of Canada. A suitor is already pursuing Maureen, and they plan to marry when Emmy will allow. Maureen is a terrific correspondent, and we write often. Of course I miss her, but she is doing very well. She and her mother started a small children's school, and so Maureen's babysitting future is not entirely put to rest.

I must admit, I am not sure what I will do with my fortune inherited from my father. But I do plan to give some of it to the servants on the farm to perhaps rebuild their cabins or do with it what they'd like. Then some of it will go to charity and to the orphan's home. But I am sure of one thing. With most of it, I will buy nice shoes and clothes and things to give to the fugitives that will hide in our home, inspiring them to keep going on the remainder of the harsh journey still ahead of them.

I have learned to submit myself fully to the One who had me in His capable hands all along, the One who lifted me from the depths of depression and made my life into something I'd never dreamed it would be. The One who had made my heart whole again with His remarkable power. I love God wholly with all my heart, and I continue to be ever thankful for His love for me. All I have to do is ask for Him, and He is there. I thank Him every day for my freedom.

The End

Lost, broken, divided, and alone,

Catherine Carey must leave her home in Charleston, South Carolina, after a terrible fire destroys everything she knows. She ventures to Saint Louis, where she must live with godparents she does not know and begin a new life. After stumbling upon a startling surprise in the home of her godparents, she is forced to contemplate her values and sacrifice her beliefs. The very roots of her being are put to the test, and it takes the friendship of a young servant, the love of a farm boy, and most importantly, the Hand of God, to lead her into the light, where she discovers herself. Through this self-discovery, Catherine's spirit is renewed and wholly transformed.

Miranda Hall lives in Saint Louis, Missouri with her family. This is her first novel, written between the ages of twelve and thirteen. Now, at eighteen, she would like to thank God for guiding her every step and all of the people that made this project possible. This is an unedited, original work straight from the heart of a little girl with a big story to tell.